Oh, i[...] man was no[...] she scanned the dear hand[...] had kissed so pleasurably just a few hours earlier. Could she bring back that man . . . ?

Impulsively Moira stepped forward, pulled his stern dark face down to hers, and kissed him soundly.

"What the devil are you playing at?" he panted against her lips. A most enigmatic smile was on her sweet, soft, rosy mouth. He shook her slightly, enough to remind her who was the aggressor in this mysterious game. And then his muscles relaxed. Aggressor? He would be lucky if he got out of this with his brains intact!

"I surrender!" gasped the major, and put his mouth back where it longed to be, against those rosy lips. . . .

Fawcett Crest Books
by Elizabeth Chater:

ANGELA

A DELICATE SITUATION

THE DUKE'S DILEMMA

THE EARL AND THE EMIGREE

GALLANT LADY

LADY DEARBORN'S DEBUT

THE MARRIAGE MART

MILADY HOT-AT-HAND

MILORD'S LEIGEWOMAN

THE REFORMED RAKE

THE RUNAWAY DEBUTANTE

A SEASON FOR THE HEART

A TIME TO LOVE

A TIME TO LOVE

Elizabeth Chater

FAWCETT CREST • NEW YORK

A Fawcett Crest Book
Published by Ballantine Books
Copyright © 1986 by Elizabeth Chater

All rights reserved under International and Pan-American Copyright Conventions. Published in the United States by Ballantine Books, a division of Random House, Inc., New York, and simultaneously in Canada by Random House of Canada Limited, Toronto.

Library of Congress Catalog Card Number: 86-91289

ISBN 0-449-21030-8

Manufactured in the United States of America

First Edition: January 1987

CHAPTER ONE

Moira Lovelace walked carefully along the muddy lane toward the village of South Littlefield on a freezingly cold morning in June. She had to watch carefully where she put her feet, lest she slip and dirty the beautiful cape she was wearing. It was of soft brown wool, lined with lustrous sable fur, and had been Herbert Lovelace's gift to his wife Candace upon the occasion of their wedding twenty-five years earlier. In addition to being something of an heirloom already, the cape was the warmest garment they owned. Mama always insisted that Moira wear it whenever she went out in chilly weather upon an errand, and today's errand was urgent: to collect the remittance that arrived each month from Herbert's eldest brother, Sir Will Lovelace.

It could not have been easy for impractical, scholarly Papa, fifth son of a minor nobleman, to adjust to the harsh realities of providing for a wife and daughter, thought Moira tenderly, grateful for even the meager three pounds per month her grandfather had begrudgingly allotted to his stupid bookworm of a son when Herbert had so rashly married the pretty daughter of his father's French chef. The unsuitability of the match aside, there was little money to spare after the older sons were provided for. Sir Giles Lovelace had been rather too prolific. By the time suitable provisions were made for his heir, commissions in the Guards purchased for the twins, and a remittance decided upon that would keep the rakehell fourth son safely rusticated in Australia, there was very little left, either of property or funds, to establish the fifth son and his charming but dowerless French wife. Banished to a cottage in an obscure village comfortably distant from Lovelace Manor, the two innocents had cared little for their straitened circumstances. Theirs was a true love match. Candace adored her Herbert, and he adored his books, his pretty wife, and his daughter—in that order.

Moira, named by her papa after the Greek Fate, had early learned that if anything, from nourishing meals to clean linen, was to be available for the use of Herbert's family, it was she who must see to it. As a result she had acquired, one way or another, a rather unusual education. Herbert had enthusiastically shared with his bright little daughter his love of ancient civilizations, so she had become familiar with the glorious literature and challenging ideas of Greece and Rome, and could even read a little in both languages. The Reverend Clarence, rector of their small parish, had persuaded Moira's papa to let him tutor the bright girl in less erudite fields, while Mrs. Clarence had invited the child into her own warm, clean house, and had shared all her housekeeping skills. Fluffy little *Maman* had added a few elegant culinary tricks that she had observed in Chef Duvall's kitchen, and introduced Moira to a delightful repertoire of operatic arias and French folk songs.

Yet it was Moira's own steady determination that had enabled her from an early age to master and then employ the homelier arts of caring for the tiny, idyllic, but hideously inconvenient cottage, and cooking the savory meals that nourished her darling, improvident parents. At the age of twenty-four, Moira had come to be considered in the village and surrounding community as a comfortable spinster—quiet, kindly, and more like a parent than a daughter to the Lovelaces. Her remarkable education was forgiven her because she made no effort to flaunt it.

Mrs. Clarence viewed her status with regret. "The poor girl is neither fish nor flesh," she complained to her husband. "Oh, the nobs will ask the Lovelaces to dinner if they need to even the numbers, or to tea because Candace is so delightfully charming, I grant you. But for all that Herbert is a Lovelace, none of the *good* families hereabouts would permit one of their sons to marry the offspring of a penniless nodcock and a servant's daughter. But by the same token, a Lovelace couldn't be permitted to ally herself with some farmer's sprout! Where does that leave poor Moira?''

While deploring her racy language, the rector was forced to agree with the substance of his wife's remarks. He himself had required time and some prayerful consideration before deciding upon the proper attitude toward the childlike, maddeningly unworldly Lovelaces. But Moira was a different proposition. Mr. Clarence had hopes that someday her noble uncle might respond to the gentle hints the rector injected every year into the routine report he made to the current head of the Lovelace family as to the careful use Moira was making of the monthly stipend so generously given her father. He had even mentioned that, had Moira not been there to remind him, the unworldly Herbert would probably have forgotten to collect the money at all!

If Clarence had only known, such indeed had been the case on this bitterly cold morning. Moira had come into the largest and warmest room in the cottage, Herbert's library, to make sure he was ready to walk down to the village. There had been several days of cold, driving rain, and comfort-loving Herbert and Candace had kept every fireplace in the house burning brightly. Moira, concerned at the rapid depletion of the supply of firewood, had sought out her papa to remind him to order more fuel when he picked up his allowance at the office of the postmistress, conveniently located in the small general store. Her rather anxious expression softened as she beheld her parents in their usual positions: Herbert at his desk, poring over a heavy volume, and Candace curled up like a kitten on the small couch before the fire, fast asleep.

Herbert glanced up at Moira with an eager smile. ''I have just discovered a most disturbing passage in Emperor

3

Justinian's *Digest of Roman Law*," he began, then frowned. "You are not here to tell me it is time for lunch already?"

Moira chuckled, shaking her head. "Papa! It is barely nine o'clock! You ate breakfast scarcely an hour ago. I came to remind you that this is the day to pick up your allowance."

Dismissing such pedestrian considerations out of hand, Herbert lifted up the volume and began to read, first explaining the case. "This refers to the torture of a slave who has insulted someone other than his master. *'Some sorts of insults might seem slight and of no importance when caused by free men, yet they are serious when inflicted by slaves, for an insult increases in the light of who it was who caused it.'* Provocative, is it not? I must arrange to discuss the idea with Clarence." Turning back to his desk, Herbert began to make notes, presumably to use during the proposed conference.

Shaking her head indulgently, Moira went quietly out of the room and took from the chest against the wall her *maman*'s beautiful cape. Whenever either one of Herbert's ladies had to go into the village in the cold weather, she would don this elegant and agreeable garment, and feel both protected from the elements and very much à la mode. Moira, mulling over her father's quotation as she made her way along the country lanes to the village, had at first chuckled at his preoccupation with ancient Roman law, and then wondered a little wryly what the barbaric custom of punishing slaves had to do with modern life. Of course there was always the *principle* of the thing. *Was* an insult less or more insulting depending upon the social position of the insulter? Surely a person of one's own class might be expected to *know better*, and must therefore be held more accountable and punished *more* severely for graceless behavior? Shaking her head in rueful amusement, Moira decided to leave such delicate distinctions to the scholar and the cleric, and proceeded upon her way, leaning into the fresh, boisterous wind, which made her glad of the fur-lined cape.

She had reached the little shop, received her father's

mail, and was enjoying a comfortable coze with Mrs. Framble, the postmistress, when both ladies heard a chorus of male cries and shouts from the street.

"Whatever are they up to now?" complained Mrs. Framble. "Farmer Jonas's bull hasn't broke out again, surely?"

"Perhaps the slaves have risen?" Moira suggested wickedly. "Being tired of extra punishment for a common crime," she explained at the postmistress's inquiring stare.

"The only slaves around here are the housewives," argued the happily widowed Mrs. Framble. "Let's go outside and have a look anyway," and she led the way.

The first thing they saw was a veritable crowd of men and women running down the street toward Moira's home. Then, to their horror, both women saw the giant plume of smoke that rose into the air beyond the village. It was wind-tossed and scintillating with fiery sparks and burning embers.

"My God," said Mrs. Framble devoutly. "That looks like—oh, *no*! Not your cottage!"

By the time Moira reached her home, it was a blazing pyre, fanned by the tempestuous wind. Mindless with fear for her parents, the girl attempted to run into the inferno, but was restrained by strong arms. And then Mrs. Clarence was beside her, pulling her close into a protective embrace, and drawing her away from the scene of disaster.

At the rectory, the good woman murmured an endless soft stream of comfort, assuring Moira that Mr. Clarence would take care of everything. Meanwhile she was removing the girl's mud-stained boots, and loosening the cape, which she tucked around the silently weeping girl as she got her into bed.

In the days that followed, the good couple did their loving best to temper the wind to the shorn lamb, and comfort Moira in her crushing loss. Mrs. Clarence, ever practical, made Moira's clothing her first concern. Since the cottage and its contents had been reduced to ashes, Moira's wardrobe consisted of what she stood up in. Fortunately she had

5

been wearing her best dress, a brown wool redingote with orange facings. Candace's cape was more than adequate, especially during the cold months, but her shoes, alas, did not measure up. They were sturdy country boots, suitable for walking in the muddy lanes, and had been originally ordered from a nearby market town by a local farmer, who donated them to the Clarences when he found they were too small. And Moira had gladly accepted them from her friend.

One look at the orphan's chemise, drawers, and petticoat the morning after the fire had sent the good dame bustling to her own well-stocked bureau for replacements. For the deeply sorrowing girl, the rectory became a true haven, and the Clarences tried hard to heal the wounds of loss.

Moira made a fitting return to her hostess. Even that meticulous housekeeper was pleased to admire the orphan's industry, willingness to help in any capacity, and proper control over her emotions. If she cried when she lay alone in the narrow bed at night, surely that was to be expected. And forgiven.

As to her culinary abilities, the rector himself was moved to applaud her skill one evening as he finished off a plate of delectable crepes.

"Learned that from your mama, didn't you, my dear?" he said, wiping his lips regretfully after the last luscious mouthful. "Your Grandpapa Duvall had a French chef, I have heard."

Since Grandpapa Duvall had *been* the French chef in the senior Lovelace's mansion, which was how Candace had met Herbert in the first place, Moira decided against replying to that question. Instead she took the opportunity to discuss her own future, inquiring whether the rector knew of any family that might need the services of a cook trained in the French style?

At that question, all the complacent good humor left the rector's face, and he advised the girl against entertaining any such dangerous notions. "For, of course, you must go to your papa's people, child! They are known and re-

6

spected here in the south of England, and anything else would be . . . quite ineligible!''

Moira disagreed. When the small floral tribute from her father's brother and his family arrived the day after the funeral, it had been accompanied by a stiff, grudging invitation to spend ''a few days with her uncle and aunt, while they found a suitable position, perhaps as companion to an elderly female relative, or—if she proved qualified— as a governess to some of the family's small children.''

Moira had been less shocked than Mrs. Clarence at this cold and businesslike formality. There had been no communication between Herbert and his brothers for years, the former having been given up by the rest of the Lovelaces as an embarrassing eccentric. Now, unwilling to discuss the coldhearted rejection her father's family had displayed, Moira let the subject drop.

Then, three weeks after her parents' burial service, she made up her mind. She had realized that she must leave the village—the county. Everyone was kind enough, but there was nothing for her here. The ladies in the great houses would be uncomfortable hiring as a servant a woman who had sat as a guest at their table. And as much as she appreciated the Christian benevolence of her hosts, she was of too independent a nature to accept charity forever. She was accustomed to looking after her impractical parents; she must now do something to support herself. It was clear to Moira that she must go elsewhere to find employment.

She informed Mrs. Clarence at breakfast the following morning that she would be leaving on the morrow to visit her mother's cousin, Lili Hassleton, in London.

The rector and his wife were forced to accept her decision, impressed possibly by the size of the wreath that had been sent by the Hassletons to the funeral service—quite the largest wreath ever seen in the village. Mrs. Clarence was certainly influenced by the fact the Cousin Lili had sent a long, warmly condoling letter with the flowers, urging that Moira visit them in London. The girl, reading parts of this missive to her hostess, had not mentioned the qualifying phrase ''after your year of mourning is over,'' knowing that the rector's wife would immediately recognize the tenuous nature of the invitation, and might even attempt to hinder her departure. *Which must not happen.*

Mrs. Clarence, in happy ignorance of the facts, spoke dreamily of a possible debut for her young friend. Moira shook her head firmly.

"I must not expect Cousin Lili to present me to the beau monde, ma'am! It would be quite ineligible!" She brought out the rector's phrase roundly. "I have no dowry, no prospect of getting one, and I am wearing black gloves."

The good woman was forced to concede the point, but she continued to argue that although there might be no social fuss made during the required year of mourning, still there would surely be many small *informal* occasions and family treats for Moira.

Tempted more than she dared reveal by that possibility, Moira said stoutly, "I shall hope to be of service to *Maman*'s cousin. Perhaps even to assist in dealing with the onerous duties facing the mistress of a large household—"

Mrs. Clarence honored this naïveté with the laughing comment that anyone who could send the most magnificent wreath South Littlefield had ever seen, could hardly be lacking an adequate staff of servants. The rector beamed his agreement.

Moira knew that much to be true. From the desultory exchange of news that had passed between the cousins, she had become aware that, unlike Candace, Lili Duvall had married prudently. Henry Hassleton was a successful merchant, who, having amassed an enormous fortune in trade, had now an avid desire to enter the rarefied atmosphere of the beau monde in the only way available to a merchant: he was determined to become the lord mayor of London!

To this end he had lately purchased a showy mansion in Queen's Square, staffed it with many servants, and—at great expense!—a butler who knew how to present his employers properly. Henry and his Lili were now trying to break into society with every trick and ploy at their command.

Lili, basically good-hearted and sensible beneath the pretentious facade Henry had urged her to assume, had kept up a faithful if random connection with her cousin Candace—mostly to boast of Henry's achievements, but there were also loving notes and costly gifts for birthdays and Christmases. Faced with the unpleasant choice of foisting herself upon either her father's reluctant family or her mother's loving, if position-hungry relatives, Moira had chosen the latter.

And she was not about to wait out a year on charity in South Littlefield, or alone and penniless in London! She would probably starve to death! The lawyer's letter acknowledging the announcement of Herbert Lovelace's death had made it clear that Papa's allowance would no longer be available for his daughter, who would shortly be suitably established as companion for an elderly great-aunt.

The rector, less prepared than his wife for Moira's sudden announcement, began to object to her decision; then, catching a minatory look from Mrs. Clarence, he changed course and agreed that it might be sensible for the girl to accept the kind invitation from her mama's affluent cousin.

"You know that Mrs. Clarence and myself wish only the best of things for you, Moira," he said with a good deal of honest sentiment. "Having known you from a babe-in-arms, and valued your dear papa's sterling scholarship! As well as your mama's—ah—charm," he concluded with a quick glance at his wife. But she was nodding agreement, and the sentimental moment was safely over.

That evening, while they were enjoying a tasty farewell dinner, the good man rose to his feet and presented Moira with a small packet. "I know you ladies have always a pound or two tucked away in your reticules for emergencies," he began jocosely. How shocked he would be, thought Moira, if he knew how pitifully few pounds I actually have!

The Reverend Clarence was going on, "However, you really must permit my wife and me to give you this small token of our friendship and the esteem in which we have always held you!" and he handed her a ticket for the stage-coach trip to London.

The following morning, much heartened by the Clarences' practical gift and by the excellent breakfast that her hostess had insisted she eat before departing, Moira mounted the London coach as it stopped briefly in South Littlefield. The village had never looked better than it did now when she was leaving it. The small cottages, the pretty gardens, the ancient gray stone church, all were gilded by the newly risen sun. Moira took it as a good omen, and greeted her fellow travelers with a cheerful smile.

"Good morning!" she said brightly. "Is is not a lovely day?"

No one replied.

There was a long, unpleasant pause. Moira had never ridden a stagecoach before, and for a moment she wondered if she had broken an Unwritten Rule for Travelers: THOU SHALT NOT SMILE AT THY FELLOW PASSENGERS; NEITHER SHALT THOU BID THEM A GOOD MORNING. Still buoyed up by the novelty and excitement of leaving the village for the first time in her life, Moira determined that no rebuff, no petty setback, should be permitted to destroy her pleasure in this Great Adventure.

She glanced around at her glumly silent companions. The coach was crowded. She had taken the only empty space, a corner near the window on the forward-facing seat. Next to her sat a farmer's wife in her Sunday best dress and shawl, who was all too redolent of her husband's business. Beyond her was a heavyset female in somber black garments. Across from *her* on the rear-facing seat was a man so like her, in build and costume, that he might have been her twin. Next to him, lounging at ease, was a tall, slender man wrapped in a military-looking cloak, a plain black hat pulled low over his darkly weathered face. A soldier home from the war? wondered Moira, noting with interest the excellent quality of the high leather boots he wore, and wondering what he looked like underneath the broad-brimmed hat.

With something of a shock, she realized that she herself was being just as intently scanned from beneath the hat brim by a pair of keen gray eyes. And then there was a

10

flash of white teeth in the tanned face, and the eyelids closed lazily, ending the scrutiny and leaving Moira feeling subtly challenged and a little breathless. Hastily she moved her gaze to the next passenger, directly opposite herself. This last passenger was a thin cleric who wore an air of pious resignation like a robe of office.

The stagecoach driver was shouting and lashing at his team now as he attempted to build up speed for the long hill called Johnson's Rise. In spite of all his efforts, the straining animals moved more and more slowly as they approached the crest of the hill. And then, inexorably, the heavily loaded coach slowed to a halt . . . and began to slip backward through the thick, soft mud on the road.

The black-clad female added her shout of displeasure to the bellowing of the coachman. Some of his curses, clearly audible within the coach, brought a pained grimace to the cleric's pale countenance. Still the vehicle continued to slip backward down the hill; the horses fought against the heavy drag of the vehicle, and the coachman rudely invoked several unfamiliar deities.

The downward drag halted; the horses strained; the whip cracked. Slowly the heavy vehicle surged forward a few feet—and then slid back again. Catching the cleric's eye, Moira ventured a smile.

"Our driver reminds one of Sisyphus, does he not?" she murmured.

The clergyman frowned. "Sisyphus?" he repeated with pedantic primness. "He who was condemned to roll a heavy stone endlessly up a hill, only to have it roll back every time?" The repressive tone of his voice made it clear that he did not approve of young females who flaunted classical knowledge more fittingly reserved for males. "I apprehend that you refer to the Greek myth of Sisyphus, Miss—uh—I am afraid I do not know your name."

"We shall have to call you Myth Sisyphus," came a mocking voice from beneath the black hat brim.

Reprehensibly, Moira giggled.

CHAPTER TWO

The crowded stagecoach jolted and swayed along the muddy road to London throughout a seemingly endless day. The disgruntled passengers had early resigned themselves to a miserable journey. It seemed to them that everything that could possibly have gone wrong with the wretched vehicle had done so, from a broken trace to a lost wheel. As a result of the recurring mishaps, the driver was several hours behind his regular schedule, and with a freshly harnessed team from the last posting-house, was straining every effort to make up lost time.

Moira was finding the endless, peevish complaints of her fellow travelers almost unendurable. She had not allowed herself to whine or complain as all the others, with the exception of the slender man, had been doing. Such self-indulgence could only weaken the shield of courage she had been building around herself since the tragedy of her parents' death. And then, when Moira felt she could not endure one more whining complaint, the cleric took a hand.

"I am the Reverend Joshua Trembly," he began in a didactic manner. "I must remind you that you enjoy the blessings of continued life and freedom from major injury. Should we not be giving thanks for these mercies? After all, we are only three hours from our destination, and there is surely nothing more that can happen to delay us—"

While his stunned hearers were wondering how to ward off the disasters such a statement would inevitably bring down upon them, the coachman, springing his horses dangerously as he rounded a sharp curve in the road, was confronted by a shocking scene. He pulled up his team so sharply that the heavy coach slewed diagonally across the road. Ignoring the screams of fear and the angry shouts from the battered passengers, Tom Coachman and his groom stared aghast at the scene of carnage before them.

A magnificent carriage had been stopped in the middle of the highway. Four men, not too clearly discernible in the fading light, were fighting a bloody battle in the road. One body, from its ornate livery obviously that of the carriage's coachman, was slumped over in the high seat. Another liveried servant had fallen near the heads of the nervous, high-bred horses. All this, Moira, from her unexpected vantage point at the window of the side-slewed coach, had taken in with one quick glance. Then her attention was caught by the central actor in the bloody conflict.

He was quite the most splendid figure of a man Moira had ever beheld. The elegance of his costume was obvious even in the dusk. He was backed against his carriage, defending himself with a slender dress sword. His three assailants were attacking him with clubs and knives. At first glance it seemed to Moira that the attacked gentleman had no chance in the world to survive. Blood flowing from his face, his clothing ripped by the knives, the defender still made shrewd use of his feet and the fist that was not holding the épée.

Moira leaned forward and swung open the door nearest her, crowding the thin cleric as she did so. There was an instant outcry from her fellow passengers.

"Wat'n'ell d'ye think yer abaut?" bellowed the burly farmer's wife. "Shut t'damn door!"

"Do you wish to see us all *killed*?" shrieked the black-clad female. "Coachman, *drive on*!"

The dialogue was resolved before Moira had a chance to answer or protest. From the shadowed woods by the side of the road came a blast of flame. *Someone had fired a shot at the stagecoach!*

This was followed by a command from the wood. "On your way, coachman! This is none of your business!"

The voice, though loud and rough, spoke with a cultured accent that surprised Moira. However, she had no time to puzzle out the inconsistency, as the frightened coachman, now reminded of his Duty, gathered the reins and prepared to edge his vehicle past the scene of battle—which, as Moira noticed, had proceeded without pause during the brief confrontation.

At that moment one of the burly attackers swung his club and connected with a dull crunch on the beleaguered hero's skull. The victim fell back against the carriage, beginning to slide down onto the road. The stagecoach driver shouted to his team, and the coach slid past the carriage.

The unpalatable fact became clear to Moira that the driver was going to obey the command of the unknown villain lurking within the shadows of the wood and abandon the embattled hero to perish in the uneven conflict! Without a single thought for her own safety, or for the gross impropriety of her behavior, Moira swung the coach door wide and half leaped, half tumbled to the road.

"For shame!" she shouted over her shoulder as she staggered through the clinging mud toward the scene of battle. "You call yourselves *men*? To let black murder be done before your very eyes, and to drive by on the other side like—like the Levite?" she challenged, recalling the Reverend Clarence's sermon last Sunday on the Good Samaritan in time to make her point.

"She's *mad*! . . . Get along, Coachman! . . . We shall all be murdered!" Wails and shouts for a speedy departure rose like a chorus from within the coach. It is possible the coachman might even have heeded them and abandoned the bedlamite to her fate, had not his groom, braver or less intelligent, at this point drawn the shotgun from its case at the side of his seat and fired off a round at the attackers, who were milling about the victim's body, kicking and thrusting.

More by luck than marksmanship, the groom peppered one of the bullies, who staggered away with a screech of pain.

For a moment there was complete silence.

Then another shot came from the woods. It was aimed at the foolhardy groom, and might have killed him had he not bent just at that instant to put another shot in his gun. The sounds and smells of flaming gunpowder, however, were an unbearable goad to both teams of horses, which immediately made the next few minutes hideous by rearing, stamping, and squalling. The groom fired off his second shot into the woods; the cleric descended slowly from the stagecoach, reluctantly prepared to help the foolish yet morally correct female. He was immediately followed by the man in the military cloak, who slid down and stood in the shadows assessing the situation.

There was a hoarse shout of command from the woods. Heeding the call, the attackers ran or stumbled or dragged themselves from the highroad into the trees. There followed the sound of horses crashing through the underbrush. The stagecoach driver looked toward his groom, ready to chide or praise depending upon how puffed up the lad was with his own valor. A broad grin lighted his face as the youth slid slowly from the seat in a dead faint.

Moira meanwhile had been hastening toward the victim of the murderous attack. She was horrified to observe, as she came closer, that not only was his face battered and bloodstained, but that a huge lump was rapidly swelling just above his forehead. She went on her knees beside the prostrate form.

"Ye gods! The brutes have killed you!" she cried, pulling her best linen handkerchief from her reticule. As she bent over to wipe the blood from his face, her eyes widened with surprise. For, though battered and bleeding the man's face undoubtedly was, he was undeniably the most beautiful human being she had ever beheld.

"Apollo!" breathed Herbert's daughter. *"Adonis!"*

The Greek god's eyes opened with agonized effort at the sound of her voice. He blinked away blood, and stared hard into the face above him. Then a grimace of pain and hatred twisted his features. *"A woman!"* he snarled. "I might have guessed a woman planned this!"

And then, most unfairly denying Moira a chance to set

15

him straight as to her complete innocence of the dastardly crime of directing the ambush—and furthermore, of her courageous decision, against rather heavy odds, to assist the victim of it—the ungrateful creature promptly fainted again!

CHAPTER THREE

The driver of the stagecoach, having convinced himself that he had handled the emergency with aplomb, was now busy lighting the small lamps on his coach. *And then I'll help the nob's groom to light his lamps, and we'll see what the damage is.* Now that the danger was safely past, Tom Coachman was perfectly willing to lend a hand to the no-doubt demoralized servants of the swell who'd gotten himself into this muddle. Urging his own dazed groom to assist, he lumbered about his task, loftily ignoring the complaints of his passengers.

Moira, torn between compassion for the wounded Adonis and annoyance at his ridiculous, unfounded accusations, became aware of presences at her shoulder. She was still crouched beside the unconscious man, using her clean handkerchief—the one her father had always laughingly called "for show" when he sent her out with two in her pocket—to wipe the blood gently from the beautiful countenance. She peered rather anxiously up at the newcomers.

One was the lean cleric, looking grim and determined. He was already luxuriating in guilt, having almost convinced himself that, had he taken charge when first the young woman had opened the coach door, much of the carnage might have been avoided. He did not stop to wonder how or what he might indeed have done to avert a tragedy already well-developed before he arrived at the scene. Now he bent toward the foolhardy female and said, with the gentle manner prescribed for deathbed comfort,

" 'In the midst of life we are in death.' " He sighed deeply. "Is there any use to offer you my assistance, miss? Is he—still alive?"

"Of course he is," snapped the woman, "and he must have immediate help, not pious platitudes! Have you any skills as a healer?"

The Reverend Trembly was forced to admit that he had not. "Solace, perhaps? Comfort in his final minutes?"

Moira turned to the other hovering figure. It was one of Adonis's servants, whose splendid livery was discernible in the light of the carriage lamps. "Well? Can you help your master?"

The fellow nodded. "We've got the lamps lighted, and I've moved Coachman inside. On the floor, I put 'im. 'E's 'opped the twig. We got to get 'is lordship to Lunnon, miss. 'E's took a rare drubbin', ain't 'e? If ye'll move aside, miss, I'll 'eave 'is lordship into the kerridge."

Moira froze. *Heave him in?* Unconscious from the terrible blow on the head, cut and bruised, and with who knew what internal injuries? Turning to the cleric, she said, "It is necessary that someone accompany this injured man to London, to protect him from being battered about any further. Are you free to do so, sir?"

The Reverend Trembly frowned. Had the woman not been listening? Masculine firmness was needed, before the creature became quite hysterical! "His servants will see him safely to his home, miss," he said repressively. "It is their bounden duty."

At this strategic moment the unconscious man stirred, groaned, and fell silent again. That was enough for Moira. "Of course, Adon—this badly wounded man cannot be shuffled into a carriage with only a dead coachman for company, and allowed to jounce about and injure himself further during a long ride over *these* roads! The groom will be required to drive the carriage. *Someone* must accompany his lordship!"

When the cleric, affronted by her aggressive behavior, merely pursed his lips, Moira accepted her fate.

"Will you please ask the stagecoach driver to remove

18

my portmanteau from the boot, sir? I shall see that Milord gets safely home.''

There was an outraged gasp from the cleric, and a ''Bravo!'' and a smothered laugh from the slender man in the military cloak, who now strode out of the shadows to stand beside the girl. Moira was pleased, in this tense moment, to have whatever support he was willing to give.

''Do you wish—that is, will you be kind enough to accompany us, and help me with Milord?'' she asked a little breathlessly. She was well aware how far she had strayed from the behavior proper for a young lady. I should have been swooning at the sight of so much blood, she thought, or screeching at the mere possibility of having to convey a terribly wounded strange man through the night in the close confines of his carriage! With the poor dead driver and another very much alive, strange man for company! Instead of which . . . but Moira dared not admit, even to herself, how much this frightening adventure, and its victim, attracted her. I must be mad, she decided, and essayed a tentative smile at the steady-eyed man.

He surprised her. In a cultured accent even the lofty patronesses of Almack's would have admired, he said gently, ''I am Hilary—ah—Sly, at your service, ma'am. It is a sensible plan you propose, and a compassionate one. Milord's family will be very grateful, I am sure.''

This judgment seemed to put a better face upon the whole ineligible scheme. Even the Reverend Trembly, while shaking his head disapprovingly, was compelled to agree that *someone* should accompany the injured man—although probably not *Miss*.

Ignoring his chiding stare, Moira swiftly assessed the problem. ''His head is injured. That enormous lump—! We must get him into the carriage without *jarring* him, if possible.''

Sly proved himself a seasoned campaigner. With the groom's assistance, he carefully removed the body of the coachman and stored it in the capacious boot. Then he helped Moira up into the carriage, straightened her soft cape about her, and made sure she was comfortably settled and ready to receive her wounded charge. Next, he and the groom lifted Milord from the road and gently eased him into the girl's waiting arms. While Moira held the massive shoulders and cradled the bloodstained head against her breast, Sly mounted beside her and lifted Milord's heavy thighs onto his own lap.

The movement attendant upon this operation brought the victim to his senses. Unfortunately, it was Moira's intent, small face, close to his own and watching for any developments, that filled the wounded man's vision.

"*You*, still?" he sneered weakly. "Do you enjoy seeing men suffer, Lucrezia Borgia? Are all beautiful women so evil?"

Although she was surprised at the thought that he found her beautiful—after all, how could he make a sensible judgment in the dark?—Moira was also angry at his persistent defamation of her character. However, this was neither the time nor the place to get into an argument, so she nodded to Sly. "I think we are ready now."

There was a flash of that white grin from her companion, who was regarding her admiringly. "Are you sure you are comfortable? He will soon become much too heavy for you, you know."

As the elegant carriage jolted and swayed into motion, Moira glanced from the tanned, smiling face of the man who had come to her assistance to the limp, bloody, disheveled male in her arms.

"He is heavy," she admitted honestly, "and I am worried about his health. Besides, I have never—that is—"

Sly gave his reprehensible chuckle. "Besides, you have never held a male body in your arms before, is that it? Do not worry, child, you are doing an excellent job."

"There is more," Moira said slowly. "He has mistakenly blamed me for his troubles. He said I had arranged the ambush, and that I was evil . . . a Borgia."

"Had you indeed arranged the ambush?" asked her companion in an interested tone.

Moira's voice swelled out indignantly. "Of course I had not! I had never set eyes on the creature until the stagecoach stopped and I saw—I saw—" Suddenly the whole

20

adventure became a dizzying whirl of blood and pain and death in the girl's head. And she swayed helplessly with the movement of the carriage.

Sly's arm, strangely strong and hard for so slender a figure, at once moved to hold and steady her. His voice gave quiet reassurance. "Breathe deeply, ma'am. Here, I shall let the glass drop, and permit fresh air to come in. Shall I relieve you of your burden?"

The draft of icy air served to shock Moira back to her senses. "It was just a momentary lapse, sir. I am better now," she said hastily. "Should you not close the window? The air is very cold, and will chill our patient. He is almost frozen as it is."

Smothering a curse, Sly slid out of his own cloak and draped it over the unconscious man, arranging it to cover the girl's shoulder also. Then carefully he took one of Adonis's hands and began to chafe it. "He is cold," Sly agreed. "And we are at least three hours away from the city." He regarded the girl with admiration. "Before then, your arms will be badly cramped, I am afraid."

"Then you must change places with me before I drop Milord, must you not? I shall cover you both with this cape of my mama's, which is lined, I may tell you, with real sable fur." Moira dredged up a gallant smile.

Catching the flash of it in the gloom, Sly stared very hard at the girl, and wished he had a better light. He'd been watching her with increasing interest during the day, admiring her calm poise in the face of the series of accidents that had quite overset the rest of the passengers. Who was this managing, self-confident little female? Had she indeed had a part in the attack? Was her air of warm concern merely a clever front to cover up a vicious scheme? In Sly's line of work, he frequently encountered both men and women who were not what they seemed to be. Was this determined, capable young woman one of the trained agents he was commissioned to trace? If so, what connection could there be with this golden-haired nobleman, whom Sly had recognized as the Marquess of Donat, a leader of

London society? Scanning the girl's pale, attractive face through half-shut eyelids, Sly pondered the question.

Moira herself was experiencing most unusual sensations, aroused by the pressure of a heavy male head against her breast, and the scent of masculine skin that rose to her nostrils as the big body in her arms gradually became warmer.

The marquess was mercifully unconscious during the long drive to London.

CHAPTER FOUR

It was very late indeed by the time the carriage drew up before Milord's London residence. The exhausted groom jumped down and ran up the stone steps to the massive front door, where he beat a noisy tattoo on the bronze knocker. The building was brightly lighted; it was evident that Milord had been expected these last several hours. The butler had the door open almost before the knocker sounded twice. There was a hasty exchange, and then the butler himself, followed by half a dozen footmen, ran down to assist their master into the house.

Sly took charge with quiet finesse. He suggested that the butler send a footman on the run to secure the services of Milord's physician. He superintended the removal of the now-feverish patient from the carriage into his home, and the dignified disposal of the coachman's body. Then, with a cautionary word as to the importance of protecting Milord's head from further jostling, Sly prepared to return to the vehicle and escort the heroine to her residence.

On the way down the steps, he encountered Moira coming up. A reluctant grin made a white slash across his darkly tanned face.

"Is the Angel of Mercy not yet done with her duties?" he quizzed gently. "The wounded hero is in good hands, I assure you."

Moira was too weary to quibble. "It is just that I shall not rest until I am certain he has survived," she explained quietly. "I shall make no trouble, I promise." She walked on, entering the large, beautiful hall just as a footman was about to close the door.

The fellow looked at her suspiciously, then shrugged, and permitted the poorly dressed female and her companion to enter. "The butler'll be down in a shake," he told them. It had occurred to him that these odd persons had perhaps rescued his master from the highwaymen, and were hanging about in hopes of a reward. He attempted to seat them on a carved bench near the door, but the female was having none of that.

"Lead me to your master's rooms," she commanded. "I wish to explain the nature of his injuries to some responsible person, and to be certain he is properly cared for."

This piece of impertinence was enough to rouse the temper of any one of Milord's superbly trained servants, but before the footman could give this saucy female a proper comeuppance, the knocker sounded again. Rolling his eyes, the footman went to answer it.

The doctor stood upon the threshold, a calm-appearing man, very well-dressed for the time of night. In fact, it was obvious he had been snatched away from a social function of some importance, as his first words made plain. "I hope this is a real emergency, and not one of the marquess's games," he said austerely. "I had to leave a houseful of guests to come here."

Sly wasted no time in social amenities or excuses. "The marquess was attacked on the highroad by four ruffians who shot his coachman to death and would have murdered Milord had not this young lady left the safety of her own coach to help drive off the villains and bring Milord safely home," he said quietly. "Your patient had a heavy blow to the cranium, a number of knife cuts, blows, and possible internal injuries. We felt it better not to disturb him more than was necessary to get him home."

The doctor's brows had drawn down heavily at this startling news. He looked from the remarkably self-possessed man to the exhausted girl. "Were either of you hurt in the—ah—melee?" he asked.

24

"Fortunately, no," said Sly smoothly. "Your butler has my direction if more information is needed than can be gotten from Milord's groom. I shall see this lady to her home as soon as she has assured herself that Milord is indeed safe and in good hands."

The doctor, who wished to attend his patient with all haste, still cast a searching glance at the young woman. Not a lightskirt, he was sure. And by her costume, not one of the elegant ladies Milord normally escorted. But there was something about her, weary and bedraggled though she was. A certain *quality*. . . .

But Moira had changed her mind. This physician was competent; Adonis's home bespoke wealth and the kind of care that wealth and position can command. Suddenly she was too tired to sit here longer, a dowd in the midst of dazzling opulence. She turned to Sly.

"I am ready to leave now," she said. "I am sure the doctor will know what to do."

Hardly waiting for the footman to open the door, Moira walked away from her wounded Adonis.

Sly caught up with her at the foot of the stairs. The weary groom-driver had had enough sense to commandeer the services of one of his fellow servants to take his place at the reins; he knew what the commoners had done for his master that night and was determined that they should at least have a comfortable journey home. So it was that Moira mounted into the elegant carriage for the second time that night, having given the new coachman Cousin Lili's address.

Sly, who had assisted her into the carriage, stood by the still-open door. "Does your hostess know you will be arriving so late? It is well after midnight, you know."

"Oh, heavens!" gasped Moira. "I cannot foist myself upon her at this hour! What am I thinking of?" She leaned forward to attract the attention of the coachman.

Sly caught her arm. "I'll speak to him for you. First you must tell me where you would prefer to go."

"There is nowhere," admitted Moira, half-distracted with weariness and indecision. "I expect I had best try to find a decent hostel, freshen up, and wait till a civilized hour to arrive at my cousin's home. Of course I must not disturb them now!''

''Will you let me help you tonight?'' asked Sly quietly. ''You have acted with compassion and grace, and no one has bothered to thank you. My home is not, I am sure, as comfortable or as suitable as your cousin's, but it will shelter you for the rest of this night, and give you a springboard from which to launch yourself into the whirl of London tomorrow.''

Sly made this odd speech with such a look of easy good humor that the exhausted girl found herself nodding agreement. The gross impropriety of spending a night in the home of a man she hardly knew did flash briefly through her mind, but she was too tired to worry. None of her family or friends would ever learn of this adventure, she was sure. Adonis, if he remembered her at all, would think of her as the female who had plotted the ambush, but luckily he did not know either her name or her destination. The Clarences were convinced she was by now safe in the home of her cousin. And the Hassletons were not expecting their guest to arrive until next year!

Moira heard herself chuckle at the surprise Henry Hassleton was about to receive. And then, relaxing into a pair of hard arms, she yawned hugely.

Sly, who had given the coachman his direction and climbed into the carriage during Moira's cogitations, laughed softly as he gazed down at the girl he held so gently in his embrace. By the time the vehicle stopped again, Moira had fallen asleep. The grinning driver fetched her portmanteau from the boot and set it beside the narrow door of the tall house set in a long row of similar unremarkable dwellings. Bobbing his thanks for a generous pourboire, he waited until Sly had the door open and the sleeping girl safely inside before he drove off.

Moira woke up as Sly was setting her down on a couch in the small lounge, which, with a dining room, constituted the ground floor of his home. ''Where are we?'' she murmured drowsily.

Sly's familiar chuckle sounded in her ear. "It is my lair, angel, where you will find every comfort your heart could desire—and no obligations."

Moira's eyes opened wide at this strange remark, and wider when she took in her surroundings—and her host, who was staring down at her with a curiously attractive smile. "But of course I must reimburse you for all you are doing, Mr. Sly—!" she began.

The man laughed warmly. "Are you Croesus? Midas? A nabob from India?" Sly chuckled at her bemused countenance. "In this wicked city, my child, you must be very careful *what* you offer to pay for—and *whom* you offer to pay!" The amusement faded from his face as he considered the tired little face turned so trustingly up to his. "You are a naive child, aren't you? Who let you traipse off to the metropolis so casually? *Do you* have any money, fledgling?"

"I have three pounds," said Moira importantly.

"Good God," muttered Sly. He stared hard into her dazed, drowsy countenance, then straightened his shoulders as though taking on a burden. "Well, we shall discuss your wealth in the morning," he said with his white, flashing smile. "Now, to bed with you, youngling! And since I do not sport a large staff of servants, it seems I must be butler, housekeeper—and lady's maid."

With that, he swung the slight figure easily up into his arms and strode up two flights of stairs before taking her into a small, neat bedroom. He deposited Moira on the single bed, lighted a lamp, and stared, frowning, around the room.

"The commode is there, child, with a basin and a pitcher full of water. Cold, but you haven't the energy to take a bath tonight anyway. Can you get out of those clothes by yourself?"

"No," said Moira honestly. "I would rather just go back to sleep now, if you please."

Sly made a sound between a groan and a laugh. Then, throwing aside his own cloak, he carefully removed Moira's muddied cape, unbuttoned and removed her redingote, and stretched the girl's docile figure gently on the bed. Next he removed the pair of boots that Mrs. Clarence had given the girl, which were much too tight, muttering a curse when he saw the swollen, reddened, small toes. Gently he draped a woolen blanket over the already-sleeping girl, and then stood staring down at her.

"What am I going to do with you?" he murmured.

Moira was too deep in exhausted slumber to hear him.

In a more fashionable section of London, Dr. John Ernest was also staring down at an unconscious figure in a bed. The Most Honorable the Marquess of Donat, his cuts and bruises bathed and anointed with curative pastes, his head bound in soothing cold compresses, was resting quietly. Dr. Ernest intended to maintain his vigil until the nobleman came naturally out of the stupor into which the blow and the subsequent pain had plunged him. Then, when Adam Donat was conscious and aware again, there would be tests to be made, and medicines given . . . and hopes that the blow to the head had done no more than temporary damage!

"I wonder who did this to you?" mused the doctor. He was well aware that his noble patient had as many enemies as he had friends. Men whose mistresses or sweethearts Adonis had casually stolen with merely a slow, smiling glance from his thickly lashed violet eyes naturally hated the golden man; rash souls who had taken umbrage at his arrogance and challenged him on the field of honor had for the most part to recuperate from their wounds at country estates or across the Channel.

Superb lover, superb swordsman, wealthy and titled and handsome beyond belief, everything had been too easy for the young marquess, who had fallen heir to his enormous estates at the age of fourteen. The dowager marchioness, his grandmother, a much-feared power in the beau monde, had done her formidable best to keep the lad on an even keel, but the adulation and greed of the ton, plus the youth's amazing beauty, had brought her efforts to naught. Adonis was arrogant, spoiled, willful—and the unquestioned leader of male London society, whenever he cared to assume the role.

Yet finally, mused Dr. Ernest, some enemy had found a way to take revenge. But who? Foolish even to ask. More than enough motive; and so far, no clues. Well, he would wait until his patient was capable of coherent thought and speech, and then ask the questions. The officers at Bow Street had been notified. The coroner's men had come to take away the body of Milord's coachman. The groom who had survived had told his tale. Because of it, the driver of the stagecoach and *his* hotheaded groom would be questioned.

As he stared down at his patient's swollen, bruised face and bound head, Dr. Ernest was grateful that a period had not been put to the life of the beautiful young man. Could that lean, dark fellow he had met in the entrance hall have been correct? Had the plainly dressed girl been a factor in saving Milord's life? Shaking his head, Dr. Ernest prepared for a long vigil.

CHAPTER FIVE

Moira woke to the tantalizing smell of coffee. Opening her eyes, she stared around the unfamiliar room. Then her glance caught the large mug on the table beside the bed, from which was arising the fragrant steam.

"Oh!" sighed the girl, reaching, grasping, blissfully sipping.

"*Oh,* indeed," a deep male voice sounded from the doorway. "You have adopted town ways very quickly, madam! Sleeping until noon! Coffee brought to your bedside! What next, one wonders? Will I be required to maid you?"

Turning toward the voice so rapidly as almost to spill the coffee, Moira beheld a person whom she recognized at once as the steady-eyed man in the stagecoach. Who had helped her deliver the stricken Adonis safely to his London mansion, her mind added quickly; and who had brought her to his own home when she needed a refuge. A warm, sweet smile quite transformed her small, sleep-softened face.

"My benefactor!" she sighed dramatically—and then chuckled.

Sly's eyebrows rose almost to meet his black hair. Then a grin of pure pleasure softened his rather harsh features. The little female had a sense of humor, and she was neither coy nor hysterical over her unusual situation. A treasure indeed! He prepared to learn more. Adopting a stern tone much at variance with his laughing eyes, he said, "If I am to hire on as your abigail, ma'am, I must know certain factual facts. Namely, your name—"

This nonsense was greeted with a delightful gurgle of laughter, as the girl drained the last of the fragrant brew and replaced the mug on the table.

"I should think your *first* requirement would be to find out if I can afford your services," she teased.

"Oh, but I know you have the wealth of the Indies at your command," jested the man. "All of three pounds, in fact! Which will get you a much-needed pair of shoes and pay your hackney fare to your cousin's home—just barely."

At once the smile faded from Moira's face, and she stared soberly at the man in the doorway. She drew a deep breath. "Perhaps you had better leave me while I wash and dress. May I meet you . . . downstairs, in fifteen minutes, sir?"

"I cannot believe that any female could accomplish the task in so short a time," teased the dark-haired man, turning away at once and closing the door behind him.

Moira's sigh of relief was a prelude to fast, competent action as she washed, tidied her hair with a brush thoughtfully supplied by her host, and donned her wrinkled redingote. Carrying the cape and shoes, she went down the stairs to the ground floor, where a smiling Sly awaited her.

"The dining room is there"—pointing—"but I am lacking the services of my chef at the moment. I thought we might eat breakfast in the kitchen, which is one floor farther down." He led the way down a narrow, twisting stairway without looking to see if she was following.

At his shoulder, Moira said, "I really cannot envision your French chef puffing up this most inconvenient stairway three or four times a day, bearing heavily laden trays! You must pay the fellow a fortune as great as mine!"

Would she never cease to amuse him? Grinning, Sly led the way into a small kitchen that seemed little used. However, two heaped plates of food sat on the heavy wooden table, steaming temptingly.

Settling into a chair, Moira asked, "*You* cooked this?

Perhaps I should hire you as my chef, rather than my abigail.''

"Don't make me an offer until you've tasted it," her companion advised her, wielding his own knife and fork in yeoman fashion.

"I suppose I should warn you," announced the girl, picking up her fork, "that my very own grandpapa was chef to a noble house, and that his skills run in the family." She glanced at Sly provocatively.

"Then *you* should have made breakfast," retorted Sly. A satisfying interval later, the two observed each other across the empty plates.

"Good, wasn't it?" boasted the man. "Now suppose we clear up the mysteries," and his expression was pleasant but determined.

"I suppose we must," agreed Moira. It had been a delightful interlude, this thoroughly preposterous adventure with an unknown man. "I am Moira Lovelace, orphaned daughter of Herbert and Candace, and I am on my way to—seek shelter with my mother's cousin, Mrs. Henry Hassleton."

Perhaps it was the slight hesitation as she spoke that caused her companion to regard her sharply. "Does your mama's cousin know you are coming?" he asked.

"She knows," asserted Moira, and then added honestly, "but perhaps not exactly . . . *when.*"

"So, she is *not* expecting you," said Sly sternly.

"She invited me, when she heard that my parents were— killed," Moira protested. "It was a most urgent and loving invitation!"

"But—?" demanded her interrogator.

"But Cousin Lili added, 'as soon as your year of mourning is over,' " confessed the girl.

"And that will be—?" Sly persisted grimly.

"In eleven months," whispered Moira. "You see, I *had* to come," she hurried to explain. "My uncle's lawyer, who was charged with forwarding Papa's allowance every month, informed me, when he learned of Papa's death, that no further moneys would be sent. I could not find work in

32

the county, and I *could not* accept charity any longer! You can see that I would have starved if I had waited eleven months to take up Cousin Lili's kind invitation," she finished with a twisted smile.

Sly smothered a groan of frustration. "I should like to offer you a position here in my household—as you see, my present chef is notable for his absence, and you tell me that cooking runs in your family. On the other hand," he added, noting the hopeful smile that had appeared on Moira's face, "there are reasons—very valid reasons—why I cannot keep you here—" He stopped her attempt to protest with an uplifted hand, adding with a smile, "—much as I might wish to! I have a very important assignment at the moment, one that requires extreme privacy, and my employer would never countenance my bringing a young lady into the middle of it." Then, unable to bear the disappointment in the girl's face, he added quickly, "That is not to say that I could not find you some respectable and satisfying work in London, if it proves necessary to do so! But first we must consider all the possibilities. *Scout the territory!* Discover whether your mama's cousin will receive you," he explained, at the girl's inquiring look.

"Oh, have you been to the New World?" inquired Moira. "I have heard that there is a good deal of scouting being done there."

"As well as a vast deal of territory," grinned the man. "No, my present work is not in North America." He regarded the small, glowing face turned up to his with more emotion than he wished to feel. Rising abruptly, he said, "To our task, Miss Lovelace! The sooner we discover your cousin's response to your arrival, the better!" He stared at Moira for a long moment. "It is essential that Mrs. Hassleton never become aware that you have spent the night, however decorously, in my home. No mention of me, in fact, should be made."

"But surely I shall have to tell *someone* what I know of the attack upon Adonis?" began Moira. "And you played an important part in the rescue. I could not have done it without you."

Sly interrupted. ''Your Adonis is the Marquess of Donat. His name is Adam Donat. Because of his—beauty, he is naturally called Adonis in the world in which he lives and moves and has his being.''

''You do not approve either of the marquess or of his world,'' said Moira, surprising the man with her shrewd appraisal of his comment.

''I do not,'' he said curtly. ''I tremble to think of what those accomplished roués who are his companions would do to an innocent such as yourself.''

Moira frowned at him. ''*Do* to me? But what opportunity will any of them have to do anything? I am scarcely likely to meet any of them—''

''I understood you to say that Adonis had charged you with planning the ambush. I am afraid he may seek revenge.''

''But that is absurd!'' Moira cried. ''I shall only have to explain that I had never seen nor heard of him before our stagecoach came upon the scene last night—''

''I hope he may believe you,'' Sly said grimly. ''He is completely spoiled, self-willed, believing only what it suits him to believe. He may decide to arrange for your punishment without even discussing with you your role in the attack.''

Moira stared at him with horror.

''You describe a monster, sir!'' she protested. ''Surely so—so . . .''

''So beautiful a human being must have a beautiful mind and soul within that glorious body?'' mocked the man, his eyes hard with disgust.

Moira looked at him, not aware that his obvious disgust was for the roué's behavior, not for her naïveté. Her own dismay and disappointment at this abrupt reversal of friendly relations was clear to see. Sly, aware of his obligation to his employer, could not permit himself to heal the breach; this little female could become much too important to him—and that must not be permitted at this stage of his work! So he said nothing.

At length Moira said quietly, ''I should like to wait upon

Mrs. Hassleton now, Mr. Sly. If you would be good enough to get me a hackney?''

Sly shrugged and preceded her out of the kitchen. So much for fun and friendship! Well, what had he expected? She was plainly infatuated with the dissolute nobleman! Of course, he would have to let her rush upon her fate, whatever it might be. His own affairs were too important to the government at this moment to permit of distractions. A naive country mouse was no business of his! But as he stumbled up the narrow staircase from the kitchen, he discovered that it was not so easy to dismiss this particular mouse from his mind. She was an innocent, but she was also a warmhearted, caring woman. And she had no idea of what Adonis and his ilk could do to her.

With a groan he realized that he would have to accept the burden—keep an eye on the valiant mouse—and make whatever explanations were necessary to his employer!

Out of long habit, he had observed Miss Lovelace and the rest of the passengers in the stagecoach during that exasperating journey. He had formed his own opinion of the girl's character and personality. He now accepted the fact that Moira had never met the marquess, but she *had* called him by the half-admiring, half-mocking name society had given its most dazzling member. Had one of Donat's many enemies planned some scheme in which Moira was to play an unsuspecting part? To the knowledgeable Sly, such an elaborate ploy was hardly justified. What had the plotter intended the girl to *do*? The stagecoach was not even supposed to be passing through those woods at that time! And Sly could testify to the unplanned nature of the various accidents that had befallen the wretched vehicle, delaying its progress.

If there was anything Sly was very sure of, it was that this young woman was quite unfit to deal with the bored, sophisticated, spoiled nobleman she seemed to regard as a helpless victim of cruel attackers. Her open countenance, made striking only by a pair of the loveliest, most innocent brown eyes he had ever seen, would surely not be judged capable of seducing a man who had his choice of the great-

35

est beauties in Europe! Miss Lovelace's manners were those of a gentlewoman, but she was too ingenuous, and lacked the calm arrogance of your true woman of the world. Sly was forced to accept that the girl was indeed no other than she claimed—an orphan on her way to find sanctuary with her mother's cousin. His duty, then, he decided with great relief, was to get her there safely.

And as for watching over her lest she run afoul of the wicked marquess? Well, he would have to see about that!

CHAPTER SIX

"Miss Lovelace," Pomfret announced, holding open the door of the parlor, where Mrs. Hassleton was despairingly shuffling an enormous pile of envelopes on an ornate desk.

Cousin Lili rose, a small, charmingly curved woman with snapping black eyes, wearing an elegantly simple day dress. She glanced sharply at her visitor and then uttered a shriek of joyous surprise as she swept forward to take Moira into an emotional Gallic embrace.

"Je suis enchantée de te voire!" she exclaimed, her happiness at the meeting obvious. She kissed Moira on both cheeks, scanning the pale, weary little face with shrewd dark eyes. "All my condolences on your bereavement, *ma pauvre p'tite!* Soon we shall speak a little of your beloved parents, and then we shall discuss your future, but for now—welcome! *Bienvenue!"*

With an arm around the girl's shoulders, Lili spoke to the hovering butler. "This is my cousin Candace's daughter, Pomfret," she explained. "What would that make her, do you know? My niece?"

Pomfret appeared pleased at the opportunity to instruct his mistress. "If she is of the collateral rather than the linear branch of your family, madam," he began with pompous relish, "it would make her your *second* cousin, while if she is of the *linear*—"

"Enough, Pomfret, *je vous en prie*!" exclaimed Lili gaily. "I shall call her Cousin Moira! Anything else is too complicated for me . . . especially at this moment!" and

37

she peered, half ruefully, half guiltily, at the untidy heap of envelopes that was sliding off the desk.

Pomfret gave the messy pile of correspondence on the carved table a knowing glance. "RSVPs, madam?"

Lili Hassleton groaned. "I shall never get to the end of them, there are so many! And I fear I may have gotten some of the names on the wrong lists!" She turned to Moira. "*You* know! Yeses in the No column. *Quel désastre!*"

It was already becoming clear to Moira that her volatile cousin could use some help. "Oh, Cousin Lili, do let me take over that task for you! I would be so grateful for the chance to repay in some small way your many kindnesses to *Maman!*"

Both her hostess and the butler stared at her. Pomfret had privately admitted to some pretty strong reservations when the girl had presented herself to his notice a few minutes earlier. A poor relation, come to hang on the master's sleeve had been his first judgment as he confronted the visitor in the Hassletons' ornately furnished front hall. The obvious value of the fur-lined cape she wore had done something to mitigate the utter unsuitability of the rest of Miss's costume. Crumpled, dowdy—and muddy! Her speech, however, in asking for an audience with Mrs. Hassleton, had displayed the proper educated accent, and her voice was low and cultured. If indeed the girl could serve some useful purpose within the household, she might prove to be an asset rather than a liability. Still, it could not be denied that she presented a sadly tag-and-rag appearance. Not quite the thing, in spite of the fur-lined cape. His stern glance directed his mistress's attention to the condition of that garment.

Catching the direction of the butler's gaze, Mrs. Hassleton scrutinized the slender figure before her. Her eyes widened. "Your *manteau, ma p'tite!* It is covered with mud!"

"There was an accident," began Moira, reluctant to get involved in a lengthy narrative and difficult explanations in front of the imposing butler. Perhaps just a hint of the spectacular would alert Cousin Lili to the fact that this was hardly a topic to be discussed before the servants. "Our

38

coach came upon a carriage being held up by highwaymen. One man was dead—!'' She uttered a carefully calculated, sobbing gasp. "Oh, Cousin Lili, I was so frightened!''

"Poor little one, you must come up to my boudoir *tout de suite*! Pomfret, coffee at once for Mademoiselle! And be sure a bedroom near mine is prepared at once for the child.''

Pomfret was already disappearing toward the servants' quarters, a footman at his shoulder, as Cousin Lili, her arm around Moira's slender waist, led the girl up the grand, curving staircase, across a noble landing from which two corridors debouched, and up a second flight almost as imposing as the first.

"The best bedrooms are here,'' Lili informed her guest with a pride that Moira found very touching. Guiding her along a wide hallway, Lili flung open a handsome door, revealing a room of almost overpowering elegance. Moira's eyes widened, and she breathed a soundless *Oh!* Her cousin watched the girl's reaction with a gamine grin. "*Mon boudoir*!'' she announced. "Pretty fancy for an apothecary's daughter, *n'est-ce pas*?'' She giggled. "If *your* grandpapa had not been so fixed upon the idea of becoming a chef, you might be living in equal splendor now.''

Moira was forced to chuckle. "Never, Cousin Lili! Even if *Maman* had inherited a fortune, my papa would have managed to mislay it—or spend it all on rare and expensive books! He was a scholar, quite uninterested in anything outside his beloved volumes.''

"Besides being a fifth son,'' added Cousin Lili, but not unkindly.

The arrival of the coffee tray at that moment proved a welcome diversion for Moira. She did not have to pretend enthusiasm for the fragrant brew that the butler poured for the ladies. Pomfret himself had brought up the coffee, since he had no intention of missing whatever developments were to occur. He had also warned the housekeeper to attend Madam and her guest. Mrs. Plum, flanked by two maids, was at the door almost before Moira had finished her first cup of the fragrant beverage. The housekeeper immediately assigned young Annie to wait upon Miss Moira, to everyone's satisfaction, and then Mrs. Plum inquired as to Miss's luggage.

The second of the maids was sent down to retrieve the portmanteau from the front hall. Cousin Lili demanded that it be opened at once, and became quite French at the paucity and poor quality of the garments displayed to her shocked gaze.

"But, of course—the fire!" she reminded herself and the servants. "Miss Lovelace has lost *everything*!" She hugged Moira remorsefully, and kissed her again. "*Ma pauvre p'tite;* we shall go to the best modiste in town as soon as you have recovered from the *bouleversement* of the highway robbery. We must pick up a few pretty costumes to replenish your wardrobe until Camille has time to make you some proper clothing"—then hastily tucking a much-mended chemise out of sight—"including some really attractive undergarments!" Flushed with pleasure and excitement, she noted the girl's embarrassed reluctance. "We owe it to your dear *maman*," she concluded, firmly. "And you *are* going to take over my wretched correspondence, are you not?"

Two hard-to-refuse reasons for her cousin's benevolence, Moira realized, but she did gently remind her warmhearted cousin that she was in mourning.

This objection was tossed aside as being quite beneath discussion. Cousin Lili informed her that Camille would have all that was correct for the sad situation in which Moira found herself.

"Since you intend taking on the onerous duties of my social secretary," Lili reminded her, "it is necessary for my consequence in the beau monde that you present an appearance completely à la mode!"

Both Mrs. Plum and Annie were nodding hearty agreement. Moira therefore surrendered to the universal goodwill with grateful thanks and a few tears. This evidence of sensibility was taken very well by her audience. Annie promptly began to blubber, and Cousin Lili was forced to wipe away a tear of her own as she embraced her young cousin.

Into this admittedly mawkish scene intruded a heavy male voice. "What is going on?" demanded Mr. Henry Hassleton, appearing in the still-open doorway. He surveyed the woman suspiciously. "Has something gone wrong about the dress you commissioned for tonight's dinner? You know how important this evening is to me, Lili!"

"Nothing is wrong, *chéri*," his wife assured him, at once all business. "The dress will be excellent, as I promised you, and the food superb! This is my little cousin, Moira Lovelace, who has come to live with us." She smiled at the girl. Then, before the frown that was gathering on her husband's heavy features could affront or frighten their guest, she added, "Moira will be dealing with all the social correspondence I have found so confusing. You know you promised me a secretary! Moira has been well-trained in all the *social skills* by her dear mother. You do recall Candace Duvall Lovelace, who married one of Sir Giles Lovelace's sons?"

Mr. Hassleton had only the vaguest knowledge of the family from which his wife's cousin had come, his Lili not wishing to puff off her connection to a chef, no matter how skillful. Certainly she had relayed no information as to the exact position of Herbert in his family's hierarchy. The scent of a title, however minor or distant, was most definitely appealing to a merchant with large ambitions, and Henry regarded his wife's guest with a more kindly eye. Lili introduced them.

Grateful for her cousin's kindness, Moira greeted her host with all the charm she was capable of. Since that was a good deal more than she herself was aware of, Henry Hassleton fell a reluctant victim—as had Sly before him.

"Come to help Lil' with her paperwork, have ye, then?" he asked in less harsh tones. He was convinced that his wife had played a clever little game behind his back to get out of a task she loathed. "Well, I suppose I must permit Mrs. Hassleton to win this trick. She's purely hopeless at the invitations, is Lili! I can only hope you're better at the job than she is.''

Frowning, he surveyed the crumpled, mud-stained little female his wife had foisted upon him. "You're Lili's cousin, are ye? What's your name again?"

Having been informed of this detail for the third time, he grunted a welcome.

This grudging acceptance quite depressed Moira's confidence, but she went bravely up to her host and gave him her hand. Her forthright action softened the merchant's original distrust slightly, and he gave her a kinder look. His French wife, who had long regarded most of the English as a cold, unloving race, planted a kiss on Moira's cheek before she took her husband's arm and led him firmly from the room.

"*Allons, mon mari!* The child must unpack and refresh herself before luncheon, and you must tell me what you wish to do about several *important invitations* that occur on the same evening.''

Delighted at this evidence of his social success, Henry allowed himself to be led away.

With the eager assistance of Annie, Moira settled her few belongings into the charming little bedroom Pomfret and Mrs. Plum had chosen for her. Annie was bubbling over with excitement at the thought of Miss Moira's new wardrobe.

"Mrs. Hassleton's got more *style* in her little finger than most of the swells in their whole heads! She'll trig you out as fine as fivepence!"

"Does my cousin go about much in society?" ventured Moira. If that was true, perchance Moira might have the chance to discover how Adonis—the Marquess of Donat, she corrected herself—had recovered from the terrible attack.

Annie was frowning. "I ain't so sure o' that, miss. The servants do say our mistress ain't part of the—uh—bong tong, if ye get my drift? Oh, there's always plenty o' invites, mind, but not the ones the master is hopin' for.'' She blushed and cast an apprehensive glance at Moira.

"I'm speakin' out o' turn, miss! It's not my place to say such things. I do beg pardon!''

Moira soothed her distress. "No, Annie, you were answering my question honestly, which I hope you will always do. I cannot be of much help to my cousin if I do not know the true situation.''

As ever, Moira's good common sense was coming to grips with the problem. Her keen mind and strong will were already planning strategies to deal with the challenge. The Hassletons' situation reminded her of the Conlays, who had moved into the neighborhood of South Littlefield a few years ago. Mr. Conlay had had a great deal of money, and had recently married a widow of a London solicitor, so the gossip went. The couple had tried for two years to wheedle their way into county society, but finally gave up and moved back to London.

Cousin Lili must not be exposed to such humiliating defeat. She and Henry were striving to gain a foothold in the most elegant, powerful, and arrogant group in England— and they were, unfortunately, certain to fail. The odds were too great. Even a country mouse knew that much! Merchants were not welcomed into the rarefied atmosphere of the nobly born. Moira recalled how the dinner-table gossip of South Littlefield had been enlivened by a story brought back by a traveler to London. It concerned a nabob, home from fabled India, who had expended thousands of pounds in a losing battle to be accepted by the beau monde. Taken up briefly as an amusing buffoon, a court jester, went the story, but never admitted into the fellowship of breeding and long-established fortune, the wretched fellow had been publicly snubbed, mocked, ostracized, and finally had retreated to the New World.

Moira clenched her fists. It appalled her to realize just what an agonizing setdown the Hassletons were inviting. Could she—could anyone—protect them from the disastrous results of their hunger to *belong*?

The girl shook her head. She would do her best to help the couple, for Lili's sake. Then, if humiliation was inevitable, she would try to soften the blow; help them pick up the pieces; even possibly find new goals less devastating than a flight to America. It was her duty and would be her grateful repayment for Lili's loving hospitality. And Moira was no raw recruit. Had she not managed house and household for her vague, unworldly parents since she was old enough to recognize clothes and dishes that needed to be washed, accounts that must be settled, hunger that must be fed—and social obligations that must be met? Setting her jaw with determination, Moira assumed responsibility for her overambitious relatives.

The first step must be to find out just what was involved in becoming lord mayor of London.

CHAPTER SEVEN

When Moira entered the breakfast room the following morning, she found an atmosphere of gloom and doom. Since she had not attended the dinner the previous evening, having successfully begged off on the double excuse of weariness and lack of suitable costume, she was unaware of the unfortunate outcome of her host's ambitious plan. As she took in the worried frown on Cousin Lili's expressive face, and the thunderous scowl on Henry's, it was clear that the evening had not produced those results that Mr. Hassleton had anticipated.

Waving away with loathing the newspaper that a footman was unwisely offering, Henry rose and stalked out of the room without so much as a word of greeting to his wife's young cousin.

Pomfret, pouring hot tea and silently indicating the buffet laden with covered dishes of hot food, followed his master out of the room.

When Moira had made her selection and had seated herself across from Cousin Lili, the frowning woman sighed and made a very Gallic shrug.

"*Hélas, ma petite!* A thousand apologies for our gaucherie! Henry behaves *comme un enfant gâté*, while I do little better!"

Thinking that Henry made a formidable *spoiled child*, Moira asked quietly, "How can I help, dearest Lili?"

"No one can help us," her cousin advised darkly. "We

45

are as good as ruined, Henry says." Then, surprisingly, she chuckled. "The dinner was a *désastre!*"

Relieved that the older woman could find some amusement in the situation, Moira begged to be given the details.

Lili smiled ruefully. "You would seek out a silver lining? Two of Henry's most important guests did not come last night—to put it in a nut, as you English would say."

"In a nut*shell*," corrected Moira gently. She could offer no balm for the cruel arrogance of the snub. It was exactly what she had feared.

"Nut, nutshell! *N'importe!* What does matter is that Henry insisted upon waiting an hour for them. He was humiliated in front of his friends and all his fellow merchants who support his candidacy for the office of alderman."

"Had the absentees declined the invitation, or were you expecting them?" persisted Moira. It was better to face the worst, and then consider what might be done to remedy matters.

"They had not done us the courtesy of replying," Lili reported grimly. "Pomfret warned me they would not be coming when I discussed the seating arrangements at the dinner table with him. He told me that to *ignore* my invitation was as good—or as bad!—as a refusal."

Worse, thought Moira. Not even the courtesy of regrets!

"I tried to warn Henry," Lili was continuing. "He brushed it off. Said the stupid wives had forgotten to reply in time, as I often do. We might have known," she concluded gloomily, "that no member of the peerage, however shiftless or *sans gêne,* would bother to boost the consequence of a cit!"

Moira, taking a steadying breath, dared greatly. "Dearest Lili, you have always been so wonderfully kind to *Maman* and me, can you let me speak freely now? Why is it so important for your husband to be accepted by the nobility? I assure you, from what little I have observed, that when such people are not insufferably arrogant, they are excruciatingly boring!"

Forced into a smile by this jaw-breaking mouthful of

condemnation, Lili explained, "Henry is trying, the more fool he, to increase his consequence in the city. And all he has done is to lower it!"

Moira shook her head. "But he wishes to be elected as an alderman, does he not? On the way to becoming lord mayor?"

Lili sighed, "It is his dream."

Moira said slowly, "Correct me if I am stupid, dear Lili, but I understand the aldermen are elected by vote of the *citizens* of each ward in the city of London." (So much Annie had told her, answering her guarded questions the previous night.) "Whenever there is a vacancy, that is," and she looked inquiringly at her mother's cousin.

Lili pursed her lips. "You would say that these starched-up noblemen Henry is courting have little to say in the matter? I suppose this may be so. Yet to be seen to be on friendly terms with the Great Ones could do no harm! Or so Henry has said." She continued to gaze consideringly at the girl. "You would say he should forget his absurd hopes of being shoulder-to-shoulder with the nobs, and pay attention to the freemen who will be doing the electing?"

Moira's warm glance offered admiration of so sensible a notion. "Exactly, dear Lili! And for a start, let us plan another dinner very soon, before the *canaille* can whisper that our Henry was routed!"

Cousin Lili broke into a delighted chime of laughter. "Oh, I like you, Moira! You have the true French *esprit*! As well as 'good English guts'—as I have heard Henry describe it," she finished with a naughty grin. Then, becoming all business, she went on, "We shall have a dinner party in one week, in honor of my charming cousin, newly arrived in the great city of London. There can be no faintest hint of politics or civic ambition in such an occasion! We shall ask only our good friends among the merchants, and their wives—and perhaps just *one* alderman and *his* wife." Her shrewd black eyes had taken on a lively glitter at this chance for a recovery from the disaster.

Moira was delighted to witness it. "Have you a suitable alderman-and-wife in mind?" she teased.

Cousin Lili nodded once, decisively. "There is one such alderman's wife who owes me a favor. Is there not an English saying: *Gratitude is the lively appreciation of favors still to come*? Yes, I think that lady will oblige me."

In the face of so much assurance, Moira could only go along gracefully with the plan for a dinner in her honor. Useless to urge a more worthy cause for a celebration, especially while Lili had that cheerful, confident look of determination. They were in agreement, after all. They both hoped to save Henry from the fatal results of his own impractical methods of attaining civic recognition, by doing the job properly for him.

Later that morning, the invitations for the dinner party in her honor neatly written and dispatched, Moira found herself faced with that same huge, untidy pile of envelopes Cousin Lili had been trying to deal with on Moira's arrival. There were not as many inhabitants in the whole village of South Littlefield as the number of persons who had penned these notes—or had required their secretaries to do so, the girl realized. Cousin Lili was right; there were too many invitations! Moira raised her large brown eyes to meet the ironic challenge in the older woman's expression.

"I have sorted these into the days on which the function is to be held," she explained carefully.

"An excellent beginning," agreed her cousin, smiling wickedly.

"Do you really wish to attend *all* of these?" Moira asked uncertainly. "There are several for the same evenings!"

"But, of course," said Lili, her gesture provocatively Gallic. "It is a sign of social favor to be harassed out of one's mind by importunate hostesses!" And she giggled.

"You are enjoying all this a great deal too much," said Moira. "If it is such a pleasure, why were you so desperate to have my help?"

"Oh, it is no pleasure to deal with the invitations," her reprehensible cousin explained. "I myself am never sure which hostesses are *de bon ton* and which are encroaching mushrooms better given a sharp setdown—"

Moira gasped. "But I know even less about the social order in London than you do!" she wailed. "How can I make the correct choices when I know nothing about any of them?"

"There *is* that," Cousin Lili agreed, smiling.

Moira eyed her sternly. Having transferred the problem to her young cousin's shoulders, Lili was taking a casual attitude toward it. "Who *would* know?" the girl demanded. "Pomfret?"

Cousin Lili was impressed by the suggestion. "But, of course!" she breathed. "Pomfret knows everything! Let's ask him."

She pulled the bell-cord, and within a very short time the stately butler presented himself. Lili came straight to the point.

"Do you know which of these invitations we should accept?"

Pomfret considered his reply. He had scanned the franks and the return addresses on most of the notes before they were brought to Madam's desk, and had a pretty sound idea. However, he appeared to reflect before he said, "I should need to see them to be sure, madam."

Cousin Lili made an expansive gesture. "Look," she invited.

There was silence in the ladies' parlor for a good ten minutes while the butler scanned signatures. The look on Pomfret's face depressed the watching women. When at length he laid down the last envelope, Lili said what all three were thinking.

"Not good, eh?"

Pomfret avoided a direct put-down. "There are a number from persons whose consequence would not add to Mr. Hassleton's," he said quietly. He dropped one invitation after another into the small beribboned wastebasket beside the desk. "*This* is from a jumped-up mushroom. *This one* is from a lady whose social ambitions far exceed her importance. And *this* one is from a woman whose sponsorship could only have a negative effect."

"In short," said Lili bitterly, "*they* are all hoping to

ride on our coattails—while *we* are hoping to ride on theirs!''

Moira and Pomfret stared into Lili's exasperated countenance. Then, irresistibly, both of them laughed. Lili, watching in disbelief, finally gave in and joined them.

Pomfret was the first to recover his poise. Never in his adult life had he so forgotten himself in the presence of any employer. He regarded the still-chuckling females with a certain benevolence. All very well to laugh, his glance seemed to say, but we have a real problem here!

Moira caught the meaning of his look first. Grasping at her self-control, she said, almost shyly. ''Would you be willing to help us, Pomfret? To guide us?''

''To keep the Hassletons from making greater fools of themselves than they have already done?'' added Lili forthrightly.

The butler scanned the two charming faces. They were bound to get hurt no matter what he did. Perhaps it was his obligation to help them avoid the worst pitfalls. He nodded gravely.

''I can try, madam,'' he replied quietly. ''But I warn you, Mr. Hassleton will not be amused.''

''We shan't tell him,'' said Lili quickly.

''We really don't need to,'' added Moira, who had already formed a pretty shrewd appraisal of her host. He reminded her of Squire Rattray in the village, who was forever nagging at his poor wife and daughters to entertain the nobs and then bringing all their efforts to nothing by insulting the reluctant guests with his loud crudities, or boring them to death with his endless monologues.

Cousin Lili was speaking. ''We've invited some of our better friends among the merchants to celebrate Miss Moira's arrival in London. Also some pleasant younger couples, and an alderman and his wife. Miss Lovelace believes we should start slowly, and build.''

Pomfret was nodding approval. ''Well thought of,'' he said. ''As I understand it, our purpose is to create an ambience of political and social good tone that may assist Mr. Hassleton toward his—ah—goal,'' he ended, not sure how much the servants were supposed to know of their master's overweening ambitions.

The grateful smiles with which the ladies greeted his tactful reference quite paid him for his restraint.

Moira went into action at once. "You have discarded the impossible invitations, Pomfret. Could you run through those that are left, and throw out all the *doubtful* ones? I'll write polite notes to them later, saying we are desolated to miss their charming event—whatever it is!—but cannot fit it into our calendar."

Pomfret's smile acknowledged good strategy. "That will be correct," he said, and sat down at the desk to sort rapidly through the remaining envelopes. Lili ran to lock the door of the parlor, so that neither master nor servant should interrupt the crucial work. Moira sat beside the wastebasket and quickly arranged all the discarded invitations according to date, the more efficiently to write the refusals.

When he finished his task, Pomfret rose with a pitifully few invitations in his hand. "These you may safely accept, madam," and he handed them to Lili.

She stared with shock at seven envelopes.

"Actually, a very good beginning," her mentor advised her. "All are respected names, and persons of goodwill. A solid foundation."

With that, Lili had to be content—for the moment.

When Pomfret had departed to perform his regular duties, Moira beamed at her cousin. "Seven!" she waved the invitations triumphantly. "That is a whole week's worth. A good start, as Pomfret says."

Lili did not appear too happy. She shuffled them ruefully. "One formal ball. Two formal dinners. A rout. Three luncheons. Paltry!"

"Not at all," denied Moira. "More can probably be done at a luncheon than at a great ball, for instance, where you see no one for more than three minutes—and your companion's eyes are searching the ballroom for more impressive company while *you* are endeavoring to impress him—or her."

Lili was forced to smile at this pessimistic evaluation.

Still, she could see the girl's point, having, now that she took time to recall them, herself endured one or two such demeaning experiences this very season. "How did you know?"

"Papa was a Lovelace," Moira reminded her cousin. "From time to time the bigwigs in the county remembered that fact. Or they were short in their numbers, and at the last moment they would invite Papa and Mama and myself to fill in." She shook her head, attempting a casual smile.

"The creatures snubbed you?" demanded Lili.

"Oh, not intentionally. I think they felt that just being at their dinner would be pleasure enough for such gape-seeds as we were, without any special civility required. You see, we were not at all modish! Nonentities, in fact. Papa could talk of nothing but his latest acquisition: some musty volume no one at the dinner had ever heard of, or wanted to! Mama was a darling, and really quite pretty, but Papa was her whole life. She scarcely spared a glance for anyone else."

Lili nodded wisely. Unsophisticated Moira might appear, largely because of her countrified clothing, absence of any maquillage, and the truly unfortunate hairstyle she adopted. Still, the girl had her wits about her, and apparently she knew the social situation from its darkest and most unpleasant angles. And she had survived experiences that might have sent a weaker spirit into retreat! "How did you handle the rejections?" she asked.

Moira considered. "I kept smiling, and stopped trying to be interesting or to make any demands. When I found myself deserted, I looked around and sought out someone else who had been ignored. If it was an older person, I offered to fetch a shawl, or a glass of ratafia, or whatever seemed suitable." She shrugged. "And if it was a younger person, a girl, I would try to find something friendly and safe to talk about."

"What?" demanded Lili, fascinated.

"Her dress, if it was really pretty. I would tell her how well it became her, and hint that a certain young man had mentioned it earlier."

52

"That would cheer her up," agreed Lili. "But if your companion was a young man—?"

Moira was becoming a little self-conscious at this inquisition. "Very much the same. A splendid coat, especially if it was a hunting pink. And then I'd mention that several young ladies had expressed the same opinion."

Lili was thoroughly enjoying this account of her cousin's ingenious manipulations. "Were there no persons with whom you could carry on a sensible conversation? About politics, or the war, or even the latest scandal in the county?"

Moira in her turn was enjoying her town-bred cousin's ignorance of county customs. "The really *serious* conversations dealt with hunting and horses and breeding lines, and who had managed to sail neatly over the worst rasper, which was generally conceded to be Farmer Dollowby's new fence. That, as I recall, was the prime topic at the last dinner party we attended. It was the general consensus that Farmer Dollowby had erected the barrier with the sole purpose of discommoding the hunt, by gad!"

Lili grinned at Moira's mimicry of the outraged riders. What a treasure the girl was! Too bad she hadn't a feather to fly with. A speculative gleam came into Lili's eyes. Could Henry be coaxed into giving his wife's cousin a dowry?

The girl was looking at her inquiringly. No use raising expectations that might never be fulfilled, thought Lili. But her chin lifted, and anyone who knew her well would have realized that Mrs. Henry Hassleton had come to a decision. In what appeared to Moira to be a complete change of subject, the older woman announced, "We have wasted enough time! We shall go to the modiste at once! We should have gone yesterday!"

Good as her word, she bustled the girl into her newly cleaned cloak and dowdy redingote, summoned her town carriage, and sallied forth to the most elegant boutique in London.

Disregarding the horrified expressions on the faces of Mme. Camille and her toplofty assistants, who were afraid that the sight of Mrs. Hassleton's companion would disgust their discriminating clientele, Lili launched into rapid French. Moira was able to catch a word or two: robbery on the King's highroad . . . killed . . . injured . . . mud . . . heroine . . . everything lost—

At this promising phrase, the eyes of the vendeuses brightened. Mrs. Hassleton, besides being one of their own—French, whatever her place of birth—was the wife of a leading city merchant, and rich as a nabob. They rallied around the distressed girl and vowed to do their utmost to present her in a style worthy of her heroic behavior— and her sponsor.

Lili enjoyed Moira's wide-eyed delight as dress after charming dress was paraded for her approval. To say nothing of dainty silken capes, and elegant little shoes, and fans and reticules and scarves. When it came to the silken undergarments in exotic shades of peach and ecru and cream, Moira lifted dazed eyes to her cousin.

"Lili!" she breathed, half in ecstasy, half in alarm.

The Frenchwoman understood both the emotions. "Do not worry about the cost, *ma petite*," she advised, sotto voce. "Mr. Hassleton will not." Because he'll never hear about it, she thought with amusement. "As for the clothing, we cannot have the future lord mayor's cousin flaunting about in rags, can we? So bad for Henry's consequence!" she giggled.

Everyone present heaved a sigh of relief, and Camille brought out her trump card with a fine dramatic flourish. It was an evening gown, but designed, thought Moira, for an enchanted night, a once-in-a-lifetime night, a night for falling in love . . . and into her mind came the image of a beautiful golden-haired youth whose pain-filled violet eyes stared up into her face with hatred.

"No!" breathed the girl, against the pain of that repudiation.

"No?" echoed every female present, staring at the little country mouse who dared to reject Mme. Camille's greatest triumph. The shocked disbelief was tangible. It brought Moira quickly to her senses.

"I did not speak of the beautiful gown, madame," she said quickly. "I only expressed my feeling of unworthiness. This lovely creation is too splendid—!"

Reassured as to the girl's appreciation of the modiste's skill, everyone began to utter soothing and complimentary words. Cousin Lili cut through the effusion. "Nonsense, my dear!" she said briskly. "We shall be going next to that part of Madame's salon where she keeps the maquillage, and where her expert assistants can transform a country mouse into a town swan."

Moira chuckled. "I should have thought that particular transmogrification would have been possible only to the deity!"

"Naughty puss!" chided her cousin, pleased at this show of spirit. The beau monde was a pitiless arena; she knew that well. And the Hassletons and their country cousin were fair game for the quizzies and the stately dames who were the arbiters of fashion. Moira would need every ounce of courage and determination she could dredge up if she were not to be destroyed.

"Take us to your coiffeuse, madame, *s'il vous plait*," she requested.

Madame Camille herself led the way.

CHAPTER EIGHT

Adam, Marquess of Donat, glared from his sickbed at the gray-haired doctor who had just frustrated his intention of getting up. It seemed to the young man that he had already been penned within the stuffy cavern of his testered four-poster bed for half an eternity. His valet, Claude, had been horrified at the injuries that could so easily have marred for life his master's handsome features, and had been hovering like a mother-hen for days, pulling the curtains to protect against drafts, offering nauseating possets, and in general rendering his master's life wretched. Dr. Ernest had forbidden access to all would-be visitors who might have lightened Adam's boredom. And now old Ernest was turning hostile toward his patient—or so Adam believed. He frowned horrendously.

This action immediately sent spasms of pain through his aching head. His eyes watered, and he gave an involuntary gasp.

Dr. Ernest noted the symptom complacently. "It will hurt worse if you don't accept my advice and give it a little longer to heal," he remarked.

"How much longer?" asked Adam, between gritted teeth.

"Two days, possibly three. And don't forget, you young devil, that I've successfully put off the magistrate's men. They've been panting at your door, eager to discover what piece of villainy you've been up to that won you such a reprisal."

The marquess glared at the doctor who had brought him into the world. "I?" he repeated incredulously. "Are you suggesting that *I* am responsible for this attack upon myself?"

"Somebody apparently felt that you deserved a lesson," prodded the doctor. His intent was not what it appeared: to mock his patient. Rather he hoped to gather some clue as to the source of this latest attack upon a young man for whom he had a sincere but well-hidden affection. Arrogant, self-indulgent, spoiled by doting society though the handsome youth might be, yet there was, beneath this dazzling shell, a real man who might somehow, someday, be brought to understand and to accept his obligations—and his capabilities. Dr. Ernest sighed, and admitted to grave concern. This was the third attack upon the marquess of which he himself had knowledge. Who was behind them?

Was it any use to ask Adam? In the past he had merely smiled and shrugged away the question. But perhaps this time, with the pain of his battered head to sober him, Adam might discuss the matter?

"Whom have you challenged lately, you young rooster?"

Adam met his intent gaze with a cynical grin. "Do you mean overtly, or just by my mere existence?"

"No use my asking? Well, whoever your enemy is, he nearly had you this time! Had it not been for the impulsive bravery of the stagecoach groom and the timely intervention of a woman, you would surely have been murdered by the hired bullies—and that I tell you honestly."

The marquess's gaze narrowed. "So. It was *not* a hallucination, then? There really was a female mixed up in that ambush?"

"From what I have been able to gather from your groom, the attack was well under way when a stage, running hours late, came upon the melee. Your groom had been knocked down when he ran to the horses' heads after your coachman was shot. When the groom came to his senses, the stagecoach was just pulling up. A man's voice from within the woods ordered the stage to proceed. Then a shot was fired from the woods, presumably to reinforce the order. The stagecoach driver had started to obey when the coach door opened and the woman leaped down. More shots were fired—your groom was dazed and cannot remember exactly what happened, except that the attack was called off by the man within the woods, and that the woman and one of her companions first bound up your head and then brought you safe home.''

"I remember her," muttered the marquess. "I charged her with arranging the ambush."

"That is absurd," objected the doctor. "A woman in a stagecoach hours behind schedule? She could scarcely have known of the several accidents that would delay the coach! If fate had not intervened, she would have been past that particular stretch of highway hours before the ambush!''

"You seem to have done your research," sneered Adam, whose head was aching agonizingly with all this argument. "I accused the woman; she did not deny the charge."

"Of course if *Adonis* has made up his mind, it is no use anyone presenting the *facts*," said the doctor with heavy irony. "I suppose you will next try to persuade yourself that it was the woman who fired the shots from the wood, and who cut you with knives and cracked your skull with a club?''

The marquess did not bother to reply, probably because even to his jaundiced view there was no truth in the latter charges. But for some reason unknown to himself, he clung to the memory of a small, intent countenance—not beautiful, no, but fascinating, and definitely involved in some way with himself. When his head cleared a little, he would remember what had made him so sure she *knew him*. He set his jaw obstinately against Ernest's quiet rationality.

"Your suspicions arise from the temporary imbalance of your mental processes," the doctor was saying. "After the heavy blow you received, it is not to be wondered at that you have these odd humors and suspicions. In time . . ."

Adam was not ready to admit that the unknown female had had nothing at all to do with the attack. She must have been involved! It *could not* have been blind chance that had brought her to his side at just that crucial moment! He looked up to meet Dr. Ernest's steady gaze.

"Just get me out of this wretched bed and I shall soon have the truth of the matter," he vowed.

Ernest knew this was his best chance to speak of weightier matters than one insignificant female stagecoach traveler. The marquess was, in a sense, a captive audience at the moment; perhaps an old friend might be able to talk some sense into him? Pursing his lips, the doctor said quietly, "This is the third attempt upon your life that I have knowledge of, Donat. And this one nearly succeeded. If you will not or cannot defend yourself, should we not make at least some attempt to discover the instigator of the crimes? *Who hates you enough to want you dead, Adam?*"

The marquess managed a tight grin. "Scores, I should think," he began lightly. Then, seeing the pained concern upon his old friend's face, he added grimly, "My heir, for one, with or without his mama's prompting. Max Hightower, who has never forgiven me for winning his estate at faro. No matter that he was a damned fool to wager his family's home upon the turn of a card! I would offer to give it back to him, but he would call me out if I impugned his integrity so deeply. *Play and pay!* That is the motto our world lives by, Ernest!" The brooding expression left his remarkable violet eyes, to be replaced by a wicked twinkle. "And then there are Evenly, and Fotriss, and Calderwell—all of whose current mistresses I . . . ah . . ."

"I have the picture," said Dr. Ernest grimly. "You are a rake, a roué, a lecher—or so you would have London believe." Ignoring the denial that trembled on Adam's lips, the doctor went on firmly, "Oh, don't try to bamboozle me as you do the whole of the ton! I know you are bored to the soul with the brittle, selfish futility of the life you lead. But I warn you, Adam, if you do not take care, you will find you are not playing stupid games any longer, because you will be dead! Is that what you really want?"

Adam rubbed absentmindedly at his forehead and winced with the resultant pain. "Why don't you permit the magistrate's men to visit me tomorrow, sir? Perhaps between us we may find the answer.''

It was foolish to ignore the repeated attempts upon his life—more of them than Ernest dreamed of. And even if, as his old friend hinted, he was sick to the teeth of elegant depravities, he wasn't yet ready to throw in the sponge! Wiser to stop the attacker, whoever he—or she—was. For there were at least two women that Adam knew of who wished him ill. The mother of his heir was the widow of his father's younger brother. Aunt Callista had always hated anyone who stood in the way of her cossetted only child, Vivian. There had been recent hints that she was attributing Vivian's less savory exploits to Adam in a nasty little whispering campaign. His family's lawyer, Mr. Beresford, had mentioned the matter privately to Adam, and suggested that his client take a firm stand before more damage was done to his reputation.

So: Callista Donat was one possible suspect in the attacks upon him.

And then there was the fashionable beauty, Lady Bedelia Camp, with a hunger for amatory conquests and a complacent husband. It had required no effort to resist Lady Bed's rather shopworn charms, but perhaps he should not have done it so publicly!

Well, then, two females hated the Marquess of Donat. Either of them might have hired the woman in the stagecoach. Adam, cursing his aching head, decided it was high time he discovered all the facts behind this latest attack, and put an end to the whole vicious business.

Four days later, Dr. Ernest permitted his patient to rise, dress, and come downstairs to a meal in the stately dining room of Donat Town House. The staff was on its toes, for the marquess was a difficult master. At times he seemed too bored to notice any of the truly remarkable efforts that were made to please him. At other times he settled with fiendish perceptiveness upon some small lapse that would normally have gone unnoticed. They were expecting the worst today, after the reports that had filtered down from

Milord's valet, Claude, and the two personal footmen who attended upon the sick man.

To everyone's surprise, Milord ordered his physician to take potluck with him. When the two men were seated, Dr. Ernest glanced around the elegantly furnished dining room with respect and admiration. The marquess, noting this, grinned cynically. It occurred to him that not even his integritous man of medicine was proof against the trappings and lure of power. Could he be persuaded, under the influence of noble surroundings and superb food, to agree with an argument he had earlier rejected? The spoiled, much-courted young nobleman, who was not used to having his opinions flouted, and did not like the experience, launched his attack while the butler was serving the first course.

Lightly touching the neat small bandage around his head, Adam said softly, "I've got it in my mind that I know That Woman from somewhere."

He took a sip of *potage madrilène* and sighed with satisfaction, interrupting himself to comment, "If it was you, sir, who prescribed my diet in the sickroom, I can only inform you that you are a British barbarian, and prescribe for *you* a course in the French cuisine!"

Dr. Ernest acknowledged this thrust with a grin, and then responded to the marquess's opening shot. "The police feel that your self-appointed rescuer and guardian angel could have had nothing to do with the ambush. Her presence on the stagecoach is attested to; she comes from a small village in the south of England; she has never been out of South Littlefield in her life—"

"Until now," Milord reminded him. "Fortuitous, don't you think, to be there just in time to oversee—or deliver!— the coup de grace? To rush immediately to the side of a man whose gross injuries would exacerbate the sensibilities of a *normal female* and send her screaming in the opposite direction? Even more damning: to greet *a man she has never seen before by a name by which he is known among his intimates!*" He eyed his companion triumphantly. "You see, I remembered! *She called me Adonis!* Does that not reek of the fish markets to you, Doctor?"

Ernest held tightly to his self-control. If the young hellion intended to go on in this manner throughout the whole meal, not even the masterpieces of Chef Berton's cuisine would keep a long-suffering physician at this table.

"Milord!" he began firmly. "The girl is well-known in her village—"

"As what?" sneered the marquess, lifting his cup and drinking down the last of the flavorful soup. "A witch?"

"As a decent girl, gently bred, lately orphaned by a fire that killed both her parents and destroyed everything but the clothing she stood in."

"Who apparently was able to acquire enough money to enable her to come to London to look for a patron." Adam was not sure why he clung to his desire to find and be revenged upon the chit. He could see that his recalcitrance was deeply offensive to his physician, but since the marquess had never had to bend his will to anyone else's preferences or prejudices in his whole life, he was hardly likely to begin now.

Dr. Ernest had put down his napkin and was facing his host with disgust. "That, sir, was a crude and quite unwarranted remark," he said stiffly.

"Then, of course, I retract it," said Adam glibly.

His old acquaintance was not appeased by such obvious mockery.

"You would be better to spend your energies upon tracking down the man who organized the ambush and fired the shots at you."

The arrival of the second course, a baron of beef, with all its accompanying side dishes plus an excellent red wine, was more than enough to distract two hungry men from an argument neither one really wished for. Two removes later, Dr. Ernest pushed away from the table.

"Enough, I thank you, milord! I shall be unable to care properly for my other patients, if indeed I can waddle out to my carriage! I admit defeat. Nothing can touch your chef's ability to tempt a sober barbarian trencherman to foolish overindulgence!"

"I'll see he receives your compliments," Adam grinned.

62

Dr. Ernest noted that he was rather white of face, and judged that the exertions of the first day out of bed had already lasted too long. "I'll just see you settled comfortably in bed before I leave," he said, his concern evident.

Adam's temper, never stable, flared at this doubt of his manhood. He thrust his own chair back from the table, forgetting his tender head. A strangled groan was wrenched from his throat.

Ernest refrained from saying "I told you so." Instead, he motioned to a hovering footman to open the doors, and assisted his fuming patient back to his bedchamber. "I shall not prescribe a drug against the pain. It may convince you that you are only human, and that I know what I am talking about when I advise you that injuries to the head, such as you received, may take weeks to heal completely, even if you obey orders."

"And if I do not?" gritted his patient.

"Then, it may be months—or you may lose your wits," the doctor informed him crisply.

There was a brief silence. Then Adam forced a glittering, white-toothed smile.

"Yes, sir, I'll be good, sir!" he whined in a passable imitation of a penitent schoolboy.

"See that you are," advised his doctor. "I am not jesting."

Ernest left his patient in bed, morosely contemplating his ill luck. He was quickly bored, and it was not at all surprising that thoughts of the mysterious female soon occupied his mind. The more he dwelt upon her too-opportune appearance, the angrier he became. Eventually he instructed Claude to send a footman to Bow Street, requiring a runner to present himself at once. It had become vitally important to Adam Donat to discover whether the mystery woman was an agent for his enemy. She *had* been involved! She had known his nickname!

And he could not get those huge brown eyes, with their lying promise of innocence and honesty and compassion, out of his mind.

CHAPTER NINE

In another, less elegant part of London, two men met in a shadowed room. Major Hilary Norman, fondly known to his intimates as Sly, was reporting to his employer. There was a lengthy pause when the report ended. Then,

"Well done," said the older man finally. "I am taking you off this business. C will handle the kill. I have another assignment for you—"

"I should prefer not to take on anything more just at the moment, sir," Sly said firmly but deferentially. "I have some—personal matters to take care of."

The older man stared hard at him.

"We have an agreement," he said at length. Too quietly.

Sly squared his shoulders. "I—I need a little time, sir."

The prime minister of England turned away. "Report when your business is taken care of," he said over his shoulder.

Sly left the room thankfully. He knew he was risking everything he had built up since he returned from the Continent and discovered what had happened to his small estate while he had been off battling the Corsican. He loved the work, he told himself. It would have been hard to settle for anything so mundane as restoring a neglected estate, even if he had had the funds to do so. Mr. Pitt's offer to employ him in secret business having to do with the welfare of England had been relayed to him by a fellow officer—a good friend from his own regiment—and gladly accepted.

He enjoyed the excitement and the danger and the feeling that he was still serving his beloved country. He had not really felt anything missing in his life, until a girl from a small village had ridden with him in a miserable stagecoach and acted with foolish courage in an unworthy cause.

The truth of the matter is, Major Hilary Norman at last admitted, that I cannot get those innocent, laughing brown eyes out of my mind! The little idiot is in real danger, whatever her role in the affairs of the notorious Adonis.

And here goes the even more idiotic Major Norman into the fray, not even sure who the enemy is!

CHAPTER TEN

The two cousins were poring over the latest issue of *Lady's Magazine* when Pomfret announced a visitor. Since Lili had instructed the butler that they were to be denied to callers until Moira's transmogrification was complete, both ladies looked up with surprise and curiosity.

"Mr. Hilary Sly, madam. He says he is Miss Moira's bosom-bow, and must assure himself she is in prime twig."

Pomfret delivered this outrageous message with a prim face, but his eyes gleamed. It was clear to Lili that Mr. Hilary Sly was a member of a class of persons Pomfret approved of. She chuckled.

"Show in the Bosom-Bow, Pomfret, and you may serve tea."

The expression of delight upon Moira's countenance reassured Lili that she had made no mistake, and the prompt appearance of a tall, slender well-dressed man in the doorway confirmed her judgment. Lili looked the fellow over with real interest. She knew herself to be awake on all suits, and she could find, at least at first inspection, no flaws in the smiling, urbane facade their visitor presented. The first thing she noted—after his dark, well-featured face with its steady gray eyes—was the quiet suitability of his costume for the occasion. This was no jackstraw, no jumped-up counter-coxcomb. This man would never offer a draft on Aldgate pump as a substitute for honest bank notes! Of course she had heard the tale of his rescue and shelter of Moira. The girl hadn't been able to resist opening the budget and revealing the whole fantastic story to her hostess.

"Just so you'll know the risks you take in harboring me, Cousin Lili," Moira had said, with a gallant if uncertain smile.

But the smile she was offering Mr. Sly at this moment was full of real pleasure. She rose, went to the visitor, and took his hand, leading him toward her cousin. "Lili, I would like you to meet Mr. Hilary Sly, my host for the night after the attack upon Lord Donat. Mr. Sly, my cousin, Mrs. Hassleton."

Lili offered her hand with a challenging stare. Bosom-bow? it seemed to say. "I bid you welcome," she said formally, "and offer my thanks for your kindness to my young cousin."

Sly met her glance with a quizzical smile. "A great pleasure to meet you, ma'am," he murmured. "Such a relief to know that my young friend has told you—everything?"

That young devil is laughing at me! thought Lili, her own sense of humor titillated.

Moira was losing patience with these formalities. "How are you, Sly? How is our victim? Have they discovered who was responsible for the ambush?"

The smile that Sly gave Moira had Lili's eyebrows rising. "So many questions, little one!" he said softly. "Which shall I answer first? I am very well, thank you," and he grinned wickedly at the girl's eager expression.

Moira chuckled. "You are teasing me, of course! You must know I am agog to learn how the victim goes on! Is he quite restored to health?"

Lili noted that Sly's expression lost its sparkle and became guarded.

"In so short a time? After the drubbing he received? That would be too much to hope for, I am sure." His voice was colorless. "Cracked heads take time to mend, you know—in real life, that is."

Moira bridled at the suggestion that she might be a romantic. "Of *course* I know a wound takes time to heal! I

67

had hoped that you might have learned how Milord goes on.''

The arrival of Pomfret and a footman with the tea tray prevented any further acerbic exchange for the moment. Over the fragrant beverage, tensions seemed to relax, and Hilary Sly addressed his hostess rather than Moira.

''The report is, ma'am, that the marquess is the testiest patient ever seen in London. Quite disrupting the household with his scolds and tantrums! You are fortunate you do not have to put up with such behavior.''

Moira began to protest against his harshness. Sly said ruthlessly, ''No, Miss Lovelace, do not attempt to argue with me. You *did* ask for information! The fact that your intervention saved his lordship from almost certain death would not weigh a feather in the balance against his rage at the pain and humiliation he is suffering. For, of course, the rumors in the ton are that the marquess was soundly trounced by a friend whose latest mistress our hero had stolen away from her protector.''

Both women were momentarily silenced by this ungarnished report. Lili was the first to speak.

''Do you believe that rumor, Mr. Sly?''

Their visitor put down his teacup and shook his head. At this moment, his greatest wish was to remove one green girl forever from the sphere of the lecherous nobleman. Still, he did not accept the current *on-dits* as the reason for the attack upon Adam Donat. Reluctantly, he said, ''No. I wish it were that simple.'' Frowning, he surveyed the two concerned faces turned to his. How many of his very real suspicions should he share with these women? Dared he reveal to the volatile pair the few facts he was sure of?

Moira helped him to make a decision. Her glance fixed on his face, she said quietly, ''I have just two pounds now, Mr. Sly. Is that enough to hire you to make sense of this mystery?''

Lili's embarrassed expostulation was hardly noticed by either of her companions. Sly felt an unfamiliar warmth in his chest. Part of it was angry resentment at the spoiled, arrogant youth who could command so much loving interest with so little effort. At war with that feeling was a powerful need to accept whatever this little charmer had to offer, to get to know her much better. . . . He caught himself up with a rueful grin, and to give himself time, he turned to offer an explanation to Mrs. Hassleton.

"When Miss Lovelace and I were conveying the unconscious marquess back to his London residence, there was a remark made—a small jest only!—that she might decide to hire my services as . . ." Even Sly's self-possession faltered under the coolly assessing stare of his hostess. With almost a gulp, he continued, ". . . as an abigail, ma'am. Miss Moira was very tired!" he offered in explanation.

Lili's French heritage disposed her to enjoy a salted story; she found this attractive male's humor acceptable. A naughty grin teased at her lips, and her black eyes sparkled.

"You correctly resisted her offer of employment, I am sure," she said smoothly. "But perhaps this offer is more *convenable*?"

Sly wished that he might unobtrusively wipe away the dew that he could feel on his forehead. What was he getting himself into? His real employer would not be pleased at any private meddling into an official investigation. And yet—! He wanted so strongly to be near his little self-appointed guardian angel to the world! Sly squared his shoulders, rose, and sketched a slight bow.

"I shall be pleased to help Miss Lovelace investigate the question of who is behind the attacks on Lord Donat," he said. "On one condition: that she herself *stays completely out of the matter*."

Moira gasped her displeasure at this masculine arrogance, but Lili was nodding agreement. "Most sensible, sir. My cousin will be too busy helping me to launch Mr. Hassleton's campaign to have time for any under-the-counter prying. Is that not so, my dear?" she challenged the girl to contradict her.

Moira was compelled to put as good a face upon her defeat as she was able, and offered Sly a smile, which he eagerly returned.

Bosom——bow, indeed! mused Lili as they sat down again. Lili poured fresh cups of tea and Sly handed around the tiny cucumber sandwiches with perfect savoir faire. In a few moments they were amiably discussing possible approaches to the problem. No casual observer would have noticed the effect Moira's new, prettier appearance was having on Sly, nor been aware of Lili's determination to secure this charming, well-dressed man for her young cousin.

Mrs. Hassleton did not deem it expedient to inform her spouse of the fact that the ladies of his household had had an unusual visitor that day. She did, however, have some other news to share that would startle her husband. Kindly deciding to allow him to recruit his strength with Cook's excellent meal before delivering the blow, she led the way into the formal dining room, where she and Moira watched, fascinated, as Henry performed his nightly gastronomic feats. When the ladies correctly offered to retire so that the gentleman might sip his port in peace, however, Mr. Hassleton displayed an uncharacteristic desire for their company at this essentially male ritual.

"I shall take my tipple to your parlor, ma'am," he told his wife firmly. "I have a few matters to discuss with you and your cousin," he added.

The ladies preceded him into the little parlor in silence. When they had disposed themselves as comfortably as possible on the heavy furniture, Henry took up a commanding position in front of the unlighted fireplace. Favoring them with a stern glance, he prepared to address his audience.

"As you are aware, Mrs. Hassleton," he began pompously, "I have an ambition to become lord mayor of London. To which end I have hired Pomfret, bought a house, and brought in too many servants, most of whom do not pay for their keep. And now we have installed your cousin as your social secretary." He twisted his lips and then took a fortifying gulp of port. "Well?" he resumed in a minatory manner, "what have you accomplished to date?"

It might have been merely an academic question, but Moira trembled for her poor cousin.

Lili smiled sweetly at her lord and master. "I have secured for you the most important invitation of the Season," she said.

When her startled husband did not respond, she relented and went on, "There may be more impressive affairs—most of which we have no more chance of attending than the dustman or the fishmonger has. But the Honorable Mrs. Barton is having a dinner for her husband, *the lord mayor*. All the aldermen will be there, and all the merchant princes of the city, and a great many members of government and other influential persons."

"You are cutting a wheedle," said Henry angrily.

"Not at all. The reason for Mrs. Barton's dinner is to support the lord mayor's charities. Everyone of any importance in the city will be present."

Henry was more impressed by Lili's announcement than he wished to admit. He said testily, "With all that mob in attendance, we shall be lost in the press."

"Not so, *mon mari*," his wife insisted, smiling. "I have managed to secure us positions at the *head table*!"

A delighted grin broke the sullen expression on Henry's face. "How did you manage that?" he demanded.

"By pledging a quite preposterous sum of your money toward those same charities," explained his wife, "*and* by hinting that you had a special project that would be to everyone's benefit!" She gave him a wicked grin. "Voilà! Head table!"

A look of horror wiped out the pleasure Lili's earlier disclosures had brought to Henry's face. "*What project?*" he demanded. "And HOW MUCH money?"

Lili named a sum which seemed, at least to Moira's village-trained expectations, incredible. Henry gasped, lost color, and drained his glass. Wordlessly he stumbled over to the bellpull and summoned Pomfret. The butler entered with suspicious promptness, already bearing a large dark-brown drink. Henry took the whisky without a word of thanks and tossed it off. Then he went to a chair and collapsed against the cushions.

While this dramatic mime was playing, Lili drew Moira aside and whispered urgently, "*You* must think of a project appropriate for the occasion, Moira. I just made up that part of the story."

Moira felt her jaw sag. "You *made it up* . . . ?" she gasped.

Her cousin nodded. "Oh, I pledged poor Henry's money, and bought us a seat at the head table. The trouble is, Mrs. Barton has some strange notion she wishes to hold the dinner in a field somewhere—a *fête champêtre*. She says the guildhall is so dingy it depresses everyone, whereas a picnic would be a charming *divertissement*. There would be a tent, in case it should rain." That should give the girl a lead—and ingratiate her with Henry! The dowry seemed closer.

There was no time for more; Henry was staring at them, his ruddy face paler than Moira had yet seen it.

"*How much* of my money did you pledge?" he asked, as though hoping he had not heard correctly the first time.

Lili told him again. "It bought us seats at the head table," she reminded him. "Cheap at the price!"

Lili sent a mischievous glance at the worried Moira. After a few minutes, Henry asked in a strangled voice, "And the—the project? What is it to be?"

"I thought I'd leave that to you," said his wife brightly.

Henry's anguished shout assaulted their ears.

"*Lili!*" He peered at her beseechingly.

"Well, Moira did have an idea," began Lili shamelessly.

Henry transferred his pleading glance from his wife to his wife's young cousin.

Moira thought desperately. "I understand that Mrs. Barton wishes to hold the dinner out in the fields," she began. "In an enormous tent."

Henry groaned aloud. "It'll never work! It's sure to rain! It always does. And it will be so cold that no one will come! All that money *wasted*!"

But Moira had had an idea. She turned to Lili. "Do you agree with Mrs. Barton that the guildhall is ugly—*dingy*, did she say?"

Lili smiled broadly. "It is *very* depressing, chiefly because no one has spent a penny upon its upkeep for years."

"Then, there is your project, Cousin Henry!" said the girl eagerly. "You have already volunteered an enormous sum of money for the lord mayor's charities." She ignored his groaning response to "volunteered." "Everyone who hears of Mrs. Barton's totty-headed plan will agree with you, sir, that London's wretched weather is sure to play us false. I imagine most people will also agree that the guildhall needs smartening up. So you offer your money—*already committed by Cousin Lili*—to fix up the guildhall so it will regain its original look of magnificence, and suggest that the dinner be held indoors, in the comfort of their own building! Everyone will bless you for helping them avoid a damp picnic. And the Hassleton name will be forever linked with the restoration of the famous and beloved guildhall!"

Both Henry and Lili were staring at the girl with dawning delight. Henry's complexion was returning to its normal ruddy hue. Lili was bubbling with satisfaction at her cousin's clever improvisation. No one need know that Lili, evolving the scheme during the last two nights, had planted all the necessary seeds.

Henry nodded happily. " 'My name—forever linked'!" he quoted softly. Then he bobbed his head decisively. "I could not have invested my blunt in any scheme more likely to get me where I wish to be," he admitted generously. "I shall be a benefactor! Nobody's likely to come up with a neater ploy!" he beamed at Moira. "I'm as good as elected, girl!" He nodded again. "I'll just get that down in writing, over my name, and submit it to the aldermen in the morning," he said, and strode out of the parlor.

"By tomorrow he'll be convinced he thought it up all by himself," advised Lili, sotto voce. "It was clever of you, child!" Her smile was warmly approving. "A superb idea!"

Moira drew a deep breath. "I don't know where it came from," she confessed. "But with the information you gave me, it seemed a possibility, at least. I suppose it was my training at managing the cottage for Candace and Herbert. I was forever being obliged to come up with last-minute solutions to problems I hadn't known even existed. My parents were forgetful," she added, smiling gently.

A pair of loobies, surmised Lili. Dreamers, leaving all the harsh necessities to this poor child! Still, it was a perfect training for the painful realities of polite society. She had determined to win a substantial dowry from Henry for this worthy girl if it was the last thing she did! Moira deserved the best the Hassletons could provide—which was, of course, a suitable *parti*!

CHAPTER ELEVEN

Adam Donat, as it happened, was also planning something suitable for the mysterious and much-to-be-suspected Miss Lovelace. The idea had come to him during a particularly painful night. As usual ignoring the advice of those who sought to help him, Adam had spent an exhausting day interviewing Bow Street Runners, in addition to a private investigator he had hired, and finally driving his curricle to the Inns of Court to consult his lawyer. It was, of course, this last defiance of cautious common sense that had left him with an agonizing headache.

Scorning to ask for the powders that would have sent him into a heavy slumber, Adam lay in his enormous bed and tried to make sense of the contradictory reports he had received. The Runners, stupid fellows that they were, had quite cheerfully exonerated Miss Lovelace from any part in the ambush.

"Stands to reason, sir," the officer said loudly, with jovial disregard for the marquess's agonizing headache, "Miss Lovelace comes from South Littlefield, a very small village where she has lived all her life. Her father was a fifth son of a baronet, and quite disregarded by his family, from all we have been able to discover. The girl stayed there until after the death of both parents in a fire, after which she stayed with the local rector and his wife until she left to come to London, to make her home with her mother's cousin, Mrs. Henry Hassleton. Miss Lovelace is well thought of in the village, sir."

"You seem to think that the admiration of South Little-field clears her of evil intent toward me," protested the marquess, realizing unhappily as he did so that he was whipping a dead horse.

"Well, beggin' your pardon, I'm sure, milord; we can't figure out how the girl could even have *heard* of you, seein' she's never been outside her village in her life! Not quite the circles you move in, sir," he added quickly, catching the anger in the marquess's expression. He took his dismissal thankfully.

The interview with the private spy John Benedict had recommended went more easily. The man's name was Nims. He was a weasel of a fellow with an oily manner. He had taken his instructions quietly and disappeared to do his job.

The visit to the Inns of Court had been almost worth the pain his ill-advised decision to drive himself there had caused him. Samuel Beresford's ancestors had served the Donats for at least four generations. The present Beresford was about forty, and a man of culture and intelligence. Also a plain speaker, as Adam now discovered.

"What's this odd bee you've got in your bonnet, Milord?" he asked crisply. "Dr. Ernest has informed me that you have been ill, and that if you do not stop bothering yourself with this problem, you may injure your brain."

"Oh, has he?" snapped Adam. "So much for the confidentiality that is supposed to exist between a man and his physician! Perhaps if some of those who are paid to solve my problems were worth their salt, it would not be necessary for me to do all the work myself!"

Lawyer Beresford stared hard at his angry client. "Why is it so necessary for you to believe that this female nonentity has dark designs upon you, milord?" he asked, and then, not waiting for an answer that his client might find it hard to give, he went on, "There are at least three persons, none of whom could have any possible connection with Miss Lovelace, who have actual reason to wish you dead."

This forthright comment halted the marquess in midti-

76

rade. "There are?" He took a slow breath. "Can you name them?" he challenged.

"I can," said Beresford. "Trusting that you will keep everything that is said in this room strictly confidential." He waited silently until Adam nodded agreement.

"Your heir, of course, is the most obvious suspect. He is a selfish, rattlebrained, vicious little ne'er-do-well, who is already pretty far under the hatches. Oh, yes, the word is around that he's in debt to half the moneylenders in town. And his mama is endlessly telling him and everyone else that he's been robbed of his consequence, and a fortune, by the wicked marquess."

"But that is insane!" protested Adam. "He's my heir until I marry and get a son of my own, but I had nothing to do with the succession! I am my father's only son, and the rightful inheritor of the marquessate!"

"You know that; I know that. All England knows it—but Vivian Donat and his mama do not *accept* it. And they both hate you."

Adam frowned. "Surely not enough to commit murder?"

"Have there been attempts upon your life?" Beresford did not wait for an answer. "*Someone* hates you enough to wish you dead. And has proved it—three times."

"You mentioned three persons," said Adam dully. Facing the fact that someone hated him enough to murder him was not a pleasant experience for the much-admired Adonis.

Beresford was continuing grimly, "There is, second, Lord Maxwell Hightower. He has been cursing you in his cups—and he is frequently in that state these evenings, I am told. He says you cheated him out of his family's estate—"

Adam rose to his feet with an oath.

The lawyer snapped, "*Sit down!* You asked for this; now you will listen to the whole imbroglio!" He waited while Adam, head pounding, seated himself. Then Beresford continued, "An officer from Bow Street delivered certain reports to my chief clerk at my request. These indicate that Hightower has been seen on at least two occasions in a tavern near the docks, conferring with three unsavory characters. The Runners are keeping an eye on them, and wished me to warn you to move carefully."

Adam said slowly, "Is there any way I can restore the estate to Max? I don't want it! I tried to urge against his wagering it, but neither rhyme nor reason can stop the stubborn fool when he gets a notion into his head. . . ." he paused, appalled, realizing the import of what he had just said.

"Exactly," agreed the lawyer. "His friends fear he will act rashly, criminally perhaps, against the man he blames for his own irresponsible folly. You see, milord, you should have *lost* that wager, not won it!" concluded Beresford with biting irony.

Adam shook his head. "Can we work out a way to restore the property? Can you get together with his lawyer and arrange something?"

"He won't love you any the better for rescuing him from his own folly so magnanimously. In fact, he will probably never speak to you again." Beresford grinned reluctantly. "I can imagine how that threat chills you! Still, it is a most generous action on your part, milord, and in time will probably be accepted as one of Donat's odd kicks, and forgiven you." He sighed and tapped on a rather grimy slip of paper on his desk.

"Which brings us to our third suspect." He paused so long that Adam glanced at him curiously. "You aren't going to like this," the lawyer said grimly.

Adam, whose headache was by this time nauseating him, almost asked Beresford not to voice his suspicions. If it was someone he liked—trusted— Better not to know?

"Who?" he asked shortly.

The lawyer spared him nothing. "Your best friend."

Adam felt his eyes opening wider. Instantly there was a rush of blood away from his head, and he felt dizzy and faint. "Not . . . not *Benedict*?" he whispered.

The lawyer nodded. "Sir John Benedict, whom you have known from Eton, Oxford, the Grand Tour, whenever!

Whose debts you have cheerfully paid upon occasion. Who *saved you* when you were set upon by footpads one night on your way home from an assignation with—"

"I remember the incident," Adam cut in. "But it was sheerest good fortune that I spotted John coming toward me on the other side of the street—"

"Was it?" challenged Beresford. "And perhaps it was just good fortune that he was near you when the girth on your saddle broke as you were going over a particularly difficult run?"

"We are in the same hunt," said Adam woodenly. Then his expression lightened. "But in each case, John *saved* me!"

"Have you forgotten the new clause you charged me to write into your will after the first 'accident'? When a shot was fired into your carriage one night?"

Adam's face went pale. "I feared Vivian might be getting impatient," he said. "I preferred that my private fortune go to my best friend." Then he scowled. "But *no one* but you and myself is supposed to know about that clause!"

"And the witnesses," Beresford reminded him. "Your witnesses."

"My cousin Raymond—"

"Is now dead," added Beresford. "But he could have talked first."

"—and *your* chief clerk," finished Adam.

"I would stake my reputation upon Waters's discretion."

"You would say," began the marquess slowly, "that Ray told John of my bequest to him? That it was *John* who arranged those—accidents?"

"Those attempts upon your life? No, I am not yet sure enough to make a definite charge," admitted the lawyer. "But it does strike me, and my investigators, rather sharply that your best friend is so often near when trouble strikes."

"I cannot believe it," muttered Adam. *"John?"*

"You would prefer to lay the blame for the elaborate, expensive, and sophisticated attacks upon a girl from a small village, a girl, moreover, who had never seen you before in her life? Milord, Dr. Ernest is right. You are not thinking straight. The attack seems to have disoriented your brain.''

Adam was minded to argue the matter. Surely the girl could have been recruited? Not all bravos were personally acquainted with the persons they were hired to destroy, surely?

An unwelcome thought struck him. Beresford was right. Adam *was* finding it necessary to believe that the woman had designs on his life. Why should this be? He had only had a pain-blurred few seconds to observe a female's large, lovely eyes staring down through the shadows into his own. How could he, a notorious womanizer who could have any female in London by lifting a finger, have been so impressed by the Lovelace creature? Why was he convinced that she was working against him? Was Beresford right? Was it a sign of incipient madness to wish to place the blame for three deadly attacks upon a girl he didn't even know?

And then it came back to him: the soft, lovely voice murmuring *Adonis*, the pet name he bore in his own circle of intimates! If he were totally unknown to her, how had she known that name?

But when, eagerly, he had recounted the incident to the lawyer, Beresford was not impressed. ''You probably mistook the word,'' he said dismissively. ''You were in bad case, from what Ernest tells me. Difficult to be sure what she said.''

All the way home, driving the curricle slowly to protect his head from further jarring, Adam brooded on the ugly disclosures the lawyer had made. Of course there were a dozen good reasons why John had been near him! They were the best of friends. Belonged to the same clubs, the same hunt. Had the same *interests*. A wicked smile tugged at Adam's sensuous lips. It was Beresford's suspicions that were insane, not his! Because the girl *had known* his nickname.

How?

There was only one way to find out. He would ask her.

* * *

It was a good thing Nims was coming today. He would tell the investigator to drop everything else, concentrate on finding out where Miss Moira Lovelace was staying in London. When Nims had located the chit, Adam would find a way to meet her. And then he would ask his questions, get his answers, and be free of the dark spell she seemed to have cast upon him.

It was odd, he mused, how important that one woman had come to be to him. And not even his mistress! He'd had a dozen who were more beautiful, and charming and witty and sensuous—and he'd forgotten them as soon as he left them. It is because she puzzles me, he told himself. Once I've solved her mystery, I'll never need to think of her again.

If he had a vagrant thought that Nims might have been better employed watching Vivian, or Max, or even John Benedict, the marquess dismissed it. He would clear up the matter of the unknown country wench who had known his sobriquet. With that small annoyance no longer niggling at him, he would be free to deal with the greater problems of the vicious heir, the disgruntled loser—and his best friend.

It struck him then that it was John who had suggested that he employ the shifty-eyed Nims. John had added the rider that he had never had occasion to use the fellow himself, but had heard from his uncle in the House of Lords that the fellow was quick, fairly accurate in his findings, and knew how to keep his mouth shut. At the time, that had seemed recommendation enough. Now, after the disquieting conversation with Beresford, the referral presented several disturbing connotations. Was Nims spying *for* him, or *upon* him? Nims had the right of entry to Adam's home, and had made use of it on several occasions. When he handed over the reins of the curricle to a footman at his own front door, Adam was in a very bad temper indeed.

A poor night's rest did not improve his mood. He was snarling at Claude over the temperature of the morning coffee when a footman announced that Nims was below, asking to see Milord. When Nims presented himself, he had plenty to report. On his own, he had located the girl

81

in the house of her cousin's husband. He had been able to determine the status of the girl's host.

"Henry Hassleton. He's a merchant. Thinks himself a nob, and he's as rich as grease. Has hopes of becoming an alderman, and may make it. Got a pack of toplofty servants, a big house, and two carriages. The girl Moira is his wife's cousin, right and tight. Couple of Frenchies, the two cousins were. Girl comes from a little one-street village nobody ever heard of. Hassleton's wife is tarting Moira up for her 'day-boo,' the servants tell me. They are all going to Mrs. Barton's charity dinner at the guildhall—"

"When is that?" Adam interrupted.

"Couple o' weeks, at least. Word is that old Hassleton is putting up the dibs for a refurbishing of the hall. About time, too. The place has looked like a barn these last few years."

Adam frowned. This was not the background of a woman who might be open to questionable employment. Had he been wrong, as everyone seemed to think? Perhaps he had imagined the little scene: the intense, *recognizing* look in the dark eyes, the whispered "Adonis!" Had he been hallucinating?

And then Nims made a comment that brought back all of Adam's suspicions in a fierce rush.

"Lovelace was not alone when she drove you home that night after the attack," he said, consulting his notebook. "Her companion was a man who claims to be called Sly. I couldn't find out anything about him. No one seems to know who he is, or who he works for, or even where he lives. He's a real clever one at covering his tracks."

"Get onto it," snapped the marquess. "I don't care what you have to spend. Hire help, if needful. I want to know all about the fellow . . . everything!"

"Well, there was one other thing—"

"About Sly?"

"No, about the girl. She didn't get to her cousin's house until sometime the next day." He grinned salaciously. "I picked up that tidbit when I stood one of Hassleton's grooms to a drink at a pub. Now, if she dropped you off here about midnight, and she and Sly left together, then it's pretty plain *where* she was playing least-in-sight till she could call on her cousin. And with whom.''

Adam felt such a surge of fury at this leering innuendo that he was frozen into momentary silence. Then he said icily, ''Get me the information I have requested. Get it fast! I don't tolerate stupidity or insolence in servants.''

Nims was plainly shocked at the rage he had unleashed. ''I'll do my best, Milord, but I'm only human.''

''I doubt that,'' said the marquess nastily.

Nims left at once, obviously preferring a less charged atmosphere.

Adam rang for Claude, who had been hovering nervously in his master's dressing room during the interview. Adam demanded to be washed and dressed at once, himself flinging off the elaborate brocaded dressing gown in which he had taken his coffee.

''See that a carriage is ready for me in five minutes,'' he ordered.

''Breakfast, Milord?'' quavered Claude. ''Dr. Ernest was most insistent—''

''To the devil with Ernest!'' snapped the marquess. ''There is a conspiracy, just as I always knew there was! Village maiden, forsooth!'' he muttered as Claude presented a crisp linen stock. ''Keeps company with some rascal who was probably hired by my . . .'' he paused, noting Claude's wide-eyed interest. ''My coat!'' grated the marquess.

''Where are you going, sir?'' asked Claude; then, catching his master's astounded glance, hurried to excuse the impertinence, ''—in case Dr. Ernest demands to know, Milord.''

''I am going to Bow Street to speak to the magistrate himself. Then I shall call upon Beresford. I am in hopes of finding out why neither of them have discovered the one essential clue in this whole imbroglio!''

Not waiting for answer or apology, Adam walked out the door and down to his carriage in tight-lipped silence.

Claude heaved a sigh of relief. If somebody had to pay for stupidity, he was thankful it would be the magistrate or the lawyer, not Claude Jenks.

CHAPTER TWELVE

After a long wait and an unsatisfactory conference at Bow Street, Adam was driven to the Inns of Court, where he demanded to speak to Mr. Beresford without delay. The clerk hurried off to the lawyer's private office, and returned immediately with the request that Milord come in at once.

Samuel Beresford was on his feet, holding a chair for his distinguished client, as Adam strode into the room. Keen eyes scanned the younger man's face.

"What has brought you out again so soon, milord?" the lawyer asked, resuming his own chair behind the massive desk.

"I have discovered an important fact about the case," began Adam coldly. "One that seems to have escaped the notice of your investigators and those at Bow Street. Our innocent little village maiden, Miss Moira Lovelace, was in the company of a mysterious fellow known as Sly—Sly!—when the stagecoach encountered the ambush of my carriage. Sly accompanied the woman in my carriage to my home, and later went off with her. She did not arrive at her cousin's residence until the following day!" So much, said his acidulous grin, for your innocent village maiden!

The lawyer stared at him in silence. After a moment he asked, "You have been to Bow Street with this bit of gossip?"

"I have," frowned Adam, not liking Beresford's tone.

"And—?" prompted the lawyer.

"It was odd," the younger man admitted. "I got the distinct impression they already knew about Sly . . . at least *something* about him, but the magistrate refused to discuss the matter with me. Put me off with some damned official obstructiveness . . . *sure Milord will understand the need for careful procedure . . . complete secrecy . . .* and ending with some pap about sending me a report as soon as the matter is resolved!" Adam was guilty of a vulgar snort of disbelief. "What do we pay the fellows for?"

"Certainly not to permit themselves to be harassed in the execution of their duty," said the lawyer, equally annoyed. "I venture to say, milord, that the officers at Bow Street know more about their business than any outsider can possibly do—"

"Even an *outsider* whose life has been threatened at least three times?" challenged Adam.

"*Especially* such an ignorant-of-the-facts, prejudiced outsider as yourself," emphasized Beresford. He passed one hand wearily across his forehead. "A number of persons have been working at this case around the clock, milord. They are uncovering some rather disturbing facts. I can only urge that you permit those who know the hazards, and are competent to deal with them, to proceed about their business unhampered by the childish tantrums of obsessed amateurs—"

That was the wrong thing to say to the marquess at this particular moment. To give Beresford credit, he would probably not have made such a sharp comment had he not been exhausted from his own private researches into the dangerous matter. But when he caught the faint gasp of indrawn breath from his client, he raised tired eyes and discovered the extent of his faux pas.

"Lord Donat," he began, in a quieter voice.

"I shall see that the obsessed amateur does not further annoy you with his childish tantrums," said the marquess with dreadful civility. "Bid you good day, Mr. Beresford."

"Wait, milord!" The lawyer stood up and took a few

steps after his recalcitrant client. "These people are vicious—truly dangerous—"

The door slammed closed behind the nobleman.

Seating himself again at his desk, Beresford penned a hasty note to the magistrate at Bow Street, sealed it, and dispatched it at once in the care of his most trusted clerk. God grant they would not find their urgent investigations hampered by a hot-tempered, willful young nobleman thrusting his way into a business where even the professionals must tread warily!

When he had ordered his coachman to return to Donat Town House, Adam sank back against the velvet squabs, fuming with anger and discomfort. He was forced to admit that Dr. Ernest might have been correct in his prognosis. The dull ache that had been constant behind his forehead for two weeks was now supplemented by occasional sharp jabs of pain down his neck. Setting his teeth, Adam tried to relax as the carriage rumbled over the streets toward his London home. He tried to take his attention off his discomfort by focusing upon the conduct of the unknown Sly and the treacherous Miss Lovelace.

What was his best course of action? It was clear the stupid fools at Bow Street would be no help, nor could he expect anything from that old windbag, Beresford. Even Nims was too slow, and had actually no real power to deal with the woman if he did prove her guilty.

A sudden jolt of the carriage over some rough cobbles sent a stab of agony into Adam's head. Senses reeling, he clenched his fists. "I'll rest today," he muttered, "and then tomorrow I'll pay a call on the damned female and force her to admit her crime! Bow Street is too lenient on these criminals!" Slightly comforted by this decision to take the law into his own hands, the marquess managed to hold on to his wits until he had entered his own room. Then he sank down onto the bed . . . and into unconsciousness.

It would have given the marquess a great deal of satisfaction to know just how often a vision of his beautiful, battered face had thrust itself into Moira's mind during the days since the ambush. It seemed to the girl that she was forever recalling how the heavy, dark eyelashes had lifted—oh, so slowly!—to reveal eyes whose pain-dulled focus sharpened into challenge as they observed her intent, concerned expression. Surely the man could not actually believe, now that he had recovered his wits, that the woman who had rescued him, held him close in her arms during that nightmare ride, and delivered him safely to his own residence in London, was also the instigator of the attack against him?

If she closed her eyes and concentrated, Moira could still feel the weight of the man's head against her breast, and recall the exciting musky smell of him—a compound of sweat and spice, brandy and road dust—that had bombarded her inexperienced senses. It seemed strange to her now, safely ensconced in Cousin Lili's mansion, that she had actually cradled society's most dazzling, recalcitrant leader in her arms for three hours. Of course, he had been unconscious the whole time, she reminded herself, and quite unaware of the unusual circumstances, and his unusual caretaker! Color rose swiftly to Moira's cheeks as she considered his reaction if he had been conscious of her during that agonizing drive. He had seemed so determined to hate her! Would they have quarreled? Could she have made him understand the true nature of their situation? Would he have thought she was kidnapping him? The first glance from those magnificent violet eyes had been a fierce accusation! Would those eyes have glowed warmly up at her if he had realized she was trying to help him?

Moira sighed and pulled her straying thoughts into more decorous paths. She had, she reminded herself, too much to do for Lili, to be frittering away her time with romantic daydreams. Her cousin had managed to involve her very deeply in the arrangements for Mrs. Barton's charity dinner. The lord mayor's wife had now agreed to permit the banquet to be held inside the guildhall, currently being cleaned and renovated, courtesy of Mr. Henry Hassleton's splendid gift.

Planning for the dinner demanded endless meetings with Mrs. Barton and her coterie of sycophants, to discuss menus and tableware, and especially the precise order of seating. The crucial matters of cleaning and refurbishing the dingy edifice were constantly passed over as less than important, compared to what quality of china should be begged, borrowed, or purchased. Moira thought her head would split after some of these sessions, held in Mrs. Barton's stuffy drawing room, overcrowded by the wives of aldermen and of every merchant prince in London.

These ladies aspired to achieve prominence in the ton by having their names connected with the guildhall dinner, yet were unwilling to volunteer for actual service. Whenever Lili or anyone else came up with a good idea, and Mrs. Barton gave it her approval, the next order of business was to nominate someone to carry out the plan. And since Moira was the youngest and least important member of the group in Mrs. B's drawing room, it became almost a ritual to smile and move that the girl be put in charge of whatever project was currently under discussion. Motion carried.

Cousin Lili's eyebrows—carefully darkened with skillful use of maquillage—rose higher and higher with each vote. Even their rather slow-witted hostess became aware that if Moira indeed accepted all the tasks they so lightly delegated to her, she would scarcely be able to bring in the dinner under three *months*, instead of the three weeks Mr. Barton had given them earlier.

At this moment, Moira rose to her feet. She was holding a list she had made of the various tasks assigned to her so offhandedly. She directed a cheery smile around the room, telling herself that this situation was really no more threatening than a meeting in Mrs. Clarence's home to prepare for the harvest festival. She drew a deep breath and plunged.

"First I must thank you all for your kindness and confidence in assigning me the task of harmonizing all your *excellent* ideas into one grand symphony of praise for the newly restored guildhall, which will do such credit to your husbands—especially Mr. Hassleton, whose generous gift made it all possible.''

Moira smiled at Lili, who was trying to suppress a grin at her cousin's high-flown imagery. *Symphony of praise*, was it? The little vixen should be running for office!

Moira had paused, ostensibly to scan the notes she had made, actually to allow the little murmur of congratulation and pleasure that had greeted her announcement to subside. Cousin Lili's eyebrows had returned to their normal position, and a private smile tugged at the corners of her lips. She herself couldn't have buttered up these pompous idiots half so well!

Moira was going on, ''I am truly appreciative of the importance of the task you have given me, and I shall try to fulfill it properly. Of course, I lack your skills at management, but I shall try to keep to a minimum my appeals to you for guidance.''

This courageous remark was also well-received.

The last thing any of these women wish for, thought Lili derisively, is to be dragged into any of the real *work* this enormous undertaking will demand! But how can the girl handle it all herself?

It appeared that Moira had an answer for this thorny question also. She had drawn on her memories of the way Mrs. Clarence dealt with the more selfish and self-important ladies in the group, those quick to criticize and slow to help. ''I know I have your consent to bring in a few trained persons to deal with the heavier tasks''—which Moira wisely did not name—''and of course I shall refer all major decisions to you, through Mrs. Barton.''

Although the last-named lady looked doubtful, the rest applauded this sensible plan, which would remove all responsibility from everyone's shoulders except those of Mrs. Barton—and serve her right if the chit was endlessly *at her* for information and guidance!

Lili was at great pains to restrain a gurgle of laughter at this wily scheme, and at once raised a gloved hand to suggest a recess in the meeting.

90

Mrs. Barton was more than ready to agree; she had to have a talk with the little upstart Lili Hassleton had brought, and find out just how many decisions the girl was planning to drop in her lap. With this in mind, Mrs. Barton gave her hovering butler the office to serve tea, and grasping Mrs. Hassleton's arm firmly, led the way to the dining room.

While the other guests filled their plates from the mouth-watering collation prepared by the Bartons' chef, the hostess proceeded to pump Lili as to her protégée's abilities.

Lili laughed lightly. "Moira Lovelace is a very responsible young woman, Mrs. Barton," she said calmly. "I venture to guess you will never hear from her until the task is completed. Satisfactorily."

This was welcome news indeed, if it could be trusted, thought the hostess. It was true the girl seemed sensible enough, had obviously done this sort of thing before, and had a proper respect for her elders and betters. It was most reassuring to recall Miss Lovelace's earlier remarks anent handling all the details herself, and bringing in experts for the difficult bits. For everything, the good dame assured herself, so long as the chit is not forever running to me with every trifling matter. And so I shall tell her!

Mrs. Barton managed to make her point of view crystal clear to both Moira and her sponsor, and then left them to enjoy the lavish repast while she went to recruit her own strength with her particular cronies. Lili sent her young cousin a glance of sparkling admiration.

"You are to be feared, my girl," she commented softly. "A female Machiavelli, no less! How easily you twisted those stupid cows about your small finger!"

"Oh, hush, Cousin Lili!" begged the girl with a glance of humorous warning. "You must not betray my devious scheme!"

This admission of connivery so delighted the French-woman that she took another of the delicious *pâtisseries* that were the pride of Mrs. Barton's chef. Nibbling delicately, she beamed at her protégée. "I shall wait until we return home before demanding a full outline of your plans for the guildhall. Now you must reward yourself for your savoir faire by sampling at least two of these divine pastries!''

CHAPTER THIRTEEN

Major Hilary Norman was finding it very hard to dismiss a certain pair of sparkling brown eyes from his mind. At the oddest times—when he was bathing or dropping off to sleep, or even eating breakfast alone in his small kitchen—he would find himself picturing Moira there beside him, and his lean, muscular body would grow warm and he would feel protective and gentle and somehow aware of a need just to be near her. This was a new and disturbing experience for a dedicated, career-minded soldier who had never, during all his adult life, permitted himself to wallow in such emotions. He told himself firmly that when they were working together on the refurbishing of the guildhall, when in fact he was seeing the little charmer every day, he would no longer be haunted by visions of big brown eyes and a soft, sweetly curved body.

It was not surprising, then, that when the Hassletons' footman brought Moira's note requesting him to wait upon her in Queen's Square, "to begin work on Cousin Henry's project," Major Norman rewarded the delighted youth with the largest tip the lad had ever received, and within half an hour a very eager Mr. Hilary Sly was knocking on Mr. Hassleton's door.

Cousin Lili, having already formed her opinion of Mr. Sly, had agreed heartily with Moira's suggestion that she arrange a consultation with the ex-soldier. Lili had also managed to recall an important engagement she could not miss, which unfortunately coincided with the visit.

"You will not mind dealing with the matter by yourself, my dear? You do have all those notes!"

Moira assured her cousin she could manage Mr. Sly by herself—and then found herself blushing. So embarrassing!

When Pomfret ushered the tall, well-dressed man into the ladies' parlor, Moira was startled by the remarkable virility which Sly seemed to wear like a dashing military cloak. She urged him to be seated, gave him her hand, snatched it away, and found herself blushing again. Too conscious of intent steel-gray eyes and a wide white smile, she seated herself and hurried into an explanation of her personal responsibilities to Mrs. Barton's committee. She outlined the changes to be made at the guildhall and handed her guest a sheaf of neatly copied notes.

He was watching her with that devastating grin.

"So I am to be your agent, executive officer, dogsbody, and general champion in the restoration of the guildhall?" he teased.

Something in his manner, warm, gentle, put her at ease, and Moira beamed at him. "It is most generous of you to allow yourself to be recruited," she said gratefully. "I only hope all this will not interfere with your own more important work!"

"More important than refurbishing the guildhall of London?" protested the gentleman, grinning wickedly. "With so major an operation on my hands, I may *never* get back to my own work!"

Moira was forced to bite her tongue, so eager was she to ask Sly what his own work was. She scanned his tall, lean figure carefully. He was dressed well, but without the panache that characterized such modish figures as the Marquess of Donat, for instance. Even after the dastardly ambush, Milord's slashed and bloodied coat had proclaimed its wearer's à-la-modality. Sly's coat was trim yet sober; not, Moira decided, as somberly professional as that of a lawyer or a doctor, and certainly nothing like a merchant's. What, then? A soldier, perhaps, out of his regimentals and wearing civilian dress? She raised her eyes to meet the man's quizzical gaze.

94

"Decided you can trust me?" he challenged quietly.

"I knew *that* the first moment I saw you," the girl surprised him by announcing. "What worries me now is that the job might be too demanding of your time and energy. Or too boring," she added honestly.

Sly chuckled. "Tell me the worst."

Fifteen minutes later he was wondering what he had gotten himself into. In addition to coordinating the cleaning, repainting, reglazing, and necessary small repairs to the ancient, enormous, and badly neglected historic edifice, it seemed he might also have to find replacements for broken or missing tableware, silverware, glasses, and even broken chairs! Regarding the little siren who had lured him into this trap with a stern expression, he said, "I hope you are not planning on having me select—and prepare!—the menu for this affair, as well as rebuilding the hall to hold it in? What was that you said about a picnic in the park? Far wiser, Miss Lovelace! No walls to repaint!"

Moira glanced through the windows at the rain that was streaming down in gray sheets outside. "Do you really think so?" she teased. "I do not!"

"It might clear up for the great occasion," offered Sly hopefully.

"*Most* unlikely, I should say."

Sly gave in with a laugh. "I can see I shall rue the day I allowed myself to assist one small angel of mercy in her thankless task," he said. "By the way, speaking of gratitude, did that fellow you rescued ever get around to thanking you for delivering him safely?"

The moment the words were out of his mouth he regretted them. The girl's soft smile became eager, and her beautiful eyes glowed like sherry. She has never sparkled like that for me, thought the disgruntled major.

"The marquess? No, I have had no word from him," Moira admitted. "Have you heard any report about how he goes on?"

"I understand he is recovering nicely," Sly said in a colorless tone that discouraged further discussion.

Although Moira wondered whence he had his information and longed for further details, she knew enough not to ask any more questions. Mr. Sly's normally smiling, darkly tanned face had taken on a set, mulish look almost identical to that Moira's papa had worn when Mama was prying into matters he did not wish to share with her. She summoned up a cheerful smile.

"We have accomplished so much today," she said brightly. "I must thank you again for your willingness to help me bear the burden. And now let us have a cup of tea, and afterward you may instruct me as to how I can help you with the work. There is money already provided by Mr. Hassleton, so you need not fear you will have to pinch pennies!"

Sharing her soft laughter, Sly regretted his unfortunate response to her question about the marquess. Why had he pokered up that way? He did not consider himself to be a sentimental man, at the mercy of his emotions, having had all such nonsense drummed out of him during his years in the army, but he discovered that he was strangely sensitive to the moods of Miss Moira Lovelace, and very apt to respond to her in ways definitely emotional! For instance, he worried over how much damage the arrogant marquess would inflict upon the darling little fluffhead if ever she became involved with him. Then there was always the chance that the attempted murderer would next time succeed. Would Donat's death destroy her?

Sly had learned from one of Pitt's secretaries about Vivian Donat and Maxwell Hightower, and even a little about John Benedict, that suave and gracious dilettante. Although why the latter should be considered a threat was not immediately available to Sly's sources. The officers at Bow Street were closemouthed and evasive, even after he had mentioned Mr. Pitt's name. If they were subalterns of mine, Sly thought grimly, they'd open up fast enough! Even so, they had told him enough to alarm him.

The question was: Should he share any of it with Moira? Having a pretty fair idea of the girl's mettle, Sly feared to impart to her the dangerous facts he had learned, lest she fly off again to the rescue. He did not want her poking around in matters that not only did not concern her, but that might result in her injury or death.

Yet if he did not tell her *something*, he was afraid she might go haring off like the greenest of recruits into the very heart of danger. Forcing himself to relax, he turned his attention back to the girl.

Moira had interpreted his scowl correctly. "You know something, probably very dangerous, but you can't bring yourself to share that knowledge with a totty-headed female," she said provocatively.

Sly regarded her with wry admiration. "'Totty-headed'?" he laughed. "*I* should never dare to make so severe a judgment of your pretty pate, poll, sconce, skull, noodle—"

"I see *a Daniel has come to judgment*—or should I say, a babblemouth?" teased Moira, delighted to engage in word games with this endearing man.

Who had now become solemn again. "You were quick enough on the mark in what you said just now about dangerous knowledge, but I cannot trust your sense of *judgment*," he said honestly—and waited for feminine bridling. He was disappointed. Moira neither raged at him for his disparagement of her good sense, nor did she attempt to wheedle anything out of him. Instead she looked at him with an open acceptance of his decision, which served her better than she knew.

"Of course, you must not betray private information," she said quietly. "It is just that it is important to me to know what hazards the marquess faces, since he is convinced I am one of the plotters against him."

Sly shook his head. "If he believes any such nonsense as that, he should be confined to Bedlam! Oh, I remember the fact that you called him by the pet name his friends have for him. And I agree that, to a man wounded and sharply beset by ruffians, such information might, at the time, seem to prove you guilty of connivery. But it has been several weeks! By now, his lawyer and the Bow Street Runners should have been able to turn up several more likely suspects."

"Have they?" demanded the girl.

"Yes," admitted Sly, his voice hard.

Moira considered this. "And you know all—or most—of what they've ferreted out," she decided. "But, of course, you can't breathe a word of it, lest it harm his lordship—"

The major was getting tired of Moira's excessive concern over a libertine who would as soon ruin her as look at her. He interrupted angrily. "—lest you go plunging headlong into matters you are quite incapable of dealing with, and get yourself killed, you little idiot!" he roared, completely losing the calm control that had so impressed his fellow officers and men during the recent war.

Moira had the temerity to grin at him.

Between feeling shocked at his own heat, and regretful of the sharp setdown he had given this darling girl, Sly experienced some difficulty in regaining his aplomb—and the upper hand in the discussion. He recalled that his superior officers had always advised that the best defense is attack. He tried that trick, reminding himself that he was addressing not a male enemy but a maddening, rash little female who might easily get herself murdered if she didn't accept direction from a wiser and older head than her own.

In desperation, Sly adopted an overbearing, smug complacence, which immediately set the girl's teeth on edge, as he said, with a condescending smile, "You really must permit yourself to be guided by those who know far more about these matters than a young woman could ever be expected to, my dear Miss Lovelace! Now shall we drop this unpleasant matter, and return to your real concern, the restoration of the guildhall? If anything definite is unearthed concerning the case of the ambushed marquess, you may be very sure I shall report it to my little employer!"

This nauseating speech (or so Sly deemed it the moment he had finished uttering it) was received by the girl with a kindness it did not deserve. Moira's tone was still pleasant as she replied, "You males have a secret brotherhood, I see. Even when you don't particularly like one another, you close ranks when a female ventures to question your

98

omniscience. Even when, as in the case of the marquess, you all manage to demonstrate the reverse.'' And now her sarcasm was obvious.

The little witch! How dared she mock him, Major Hilary Norman, Guards officer and special agent for Prime Minister William Pitt? Why the devil was she so concerned over a lecherous brute of a nobleman she didn't even know? Out of anger and a jealousy he refused to acknowledge, Sly spoke too quickly.

"At least *I* have more sense than to be taken in by a handsome body and a pair of purple eyes!'' he snapped.

Moira stopped smiling. She searched the dark, closed countenance, seeing only cold condemnation.

"You are right, of course.'' She spoke in a dead little voice that quite pierced Sly's suddenly remorseful heart. "How could a female who had never left the confines of her village have enough sense to deal with important matters like male treachery and villainy? You will have to forgive me for thinking I might understand or help in men's *important business*.''

Sly, horrified and regretful at what he had accomplished, made a desperate effort to come about. The sight of that small, hurt face was doing uncomfortable things to him. He took a deep breath and plunged in, all desire to attack abandoned.

"I beg your pardon,'' he said, his face stained dark-red with embarrassment and something more. "I spoke foolishly, out of anger at the idea that you might get yourself badly hurt while trying to protect that—er—the marquess. He is really unworthy of your concern . . . that is—'' Sly took a deep breath. He was aware, from the expression on Moira's face, that he was plunging deeper into the moat rather than scaling the walls. The girl's huge brown eyes, still gazing at him with that *lost* expression, brought the man to his knees. Sly surrendered, foot, horse, and guns.

"Please forgive me,'' he begged. "I—worry about you, Moira.''

Oh, splendid! jibed a small voice somewhere deep in his mind. A truly masterly attack! Wellington would be proud of you! But, strangely enough, his abject surrender evoked neither scornful anger nor mocking laughter from the victor, but instead a most delightful smile of forgiveness.

"So that is why you act so knaggy every time I so much as mention Lord Donat's name," she said, as one making an important discovery. Her smile became even warmer; the man basked in the delightful glow of it, wondering at his luck. "I know exactly how you feel," Moira went on. "I myself am perhaps too strongly swayed by concern for those I care for. I was forever on the fret over Papa, who, once he got his nose in a book, could never remember to come to meals, or to attend a dinner given in honor of the squire, or even to bring a nosegay to Mama upon her birthday or their anniversary!" She beamed at him. "Most natural! How lucky I am to be included in your compassion! Now *you* must forgive *me* for being such a termagant, Mr. Sly! If I give you my word that I shall not interfere in men's work, will you in turn trust me with some of the facts? Even though they are alarming, that will be easier to bear than total ignorance of the dangers you will be facing as you work to protect his lordship. One calls up fearful images when one does not know the true facts."

Heartened by the knowledge that some, at least, of Miss Lovelace's fears were for his own safety, Sly proceeded to brief Moira upon the more-widely known threats to Milord's person. The young woman would already have known of them, and half a hundred more, both real and imagined, if she had been a member of the beau monde in which the marquess moved. As it was, even the bits of information he felt it permissible to share with her had her frowning and biting at her soft lower lip in a manner that quite fascinated the soldier.

Moira heard him out with a sober expression. At the end of the recital she asked quietly, "What had I best do? Oh, I know I must not interfere directly in a situation so fraught with danger, and I do understand that Bow Street and other proper authorities are working upon the problem, but *you* must understand that I do not wish to be thought a part of any conspiracy against the marquess. From what you have

100

said, and from my own brief contact with him,'' recalling the big, warm body in her arms, Moira blushed again, ''I am sure he links me with his vicious attackers.''

Sly was forced to admit the accuracy of this assumption, yet the only resolution he could think of, which was for Miss Lovelace to wait upon the marquess at Donat Town House and present her case, was for some reason extremely distasteful to him. While he mulled the matter, frowning, Moira was doing some mulling of her own.

For one thing, she was forced to reassess her opinion of her companion. He had shown sensitivity and concern as well as the cold anger that so deflated her. Watching him as he frowned over the best course to take out of their dilemma, the girl saw as if for the first time the tall, well-set-up man with the deeply tanned features. She had lightly dismissed him as being slender and unremarkable. She now realized that the slenderness was a lean whipcord strength without an ounce of fat or flab. The steel-gray glance could soften and warm into a sort of silver glow when Sly was moved by gentler emotions of caring and concern. And as she could testify, when the *unremarkable* man got angry, he became very impressive indeed—frightening, in fact! Moira was learning to evaluate the mysterious male sex upon entirely new levels.

There was still the provocative question of the real occupation of Mr. Sly, protector of rash females, executive officer to guildhall restorers, but regretfully Moira set it aside in order to deal with the more urgent problem of the menaced—and vengeful—peer.

''It has been three weeks since the ambush, and Bow Street has not been able to identify the culprits,'' she complained.

''How do you know that?'' Sly challenged her. ''Do the Runners report to you? Why should they?''

Ignoring this childish remark, Moira said, ''We should have heard something definite if they had found the villain.''

Sly grinned at her naïveté. ''Should *we*, indeed? Do you

not think the principals in this affair are important enough to hush up a scandal?''

"You are reminding me—again!—that I am nothing but a country mouse," began the girl with rising irritation.

"I am informing you—*again*—that the apprehension of powerful, ruthless, well-born criminals is no business of yours!" The beleaguered soldier heard his voice rising again. He set his jaw. This was like a damned seesaw! Just when he thought he had her calmed down and friendly, her fiery temper flared again! And he knew exactly why it kept happening. She was still mooning over that damned lecher!

"Why can you not permit the proper authorities to do the work they are trained for?" he burst out, exasperated.

"Because they aren't doing it!" snapped the girl.

They exchanged glares like two childish antagonists.

Suddenly seeing the humor of it, Sly laughed. His stern professional stance softened into affectionate amusement. "You are a regular little firebrand, aren't you? You look about ten-years-old, scowling so horrendously at me! You need not be afraid, dear child! I have constituted myself your protector as well as your dogsbody, and shall make personally sure that the bullyboys of the wicked marquess and his enemies do not hurt you."

Then, observing the battle between outrage and curiosity on her expressive little face, Sly continued gently, "I have arranged with Bow Street that there will be an officer on watch during the whole twenty-four hours of the day. Oh, quite unobtrusively, of course, in suitable disguise. We have no wish to draw public attention to your—connection with the naughty marquess."

Smiling, Sly waited for her thanks. In vain.

Deeply affronted by his mocking dismissal of her as a— what had he said?—scowling ten-year-old, who, it now appeared, needed a nursemaid, Moira completely failed to notice the affection in his voice and manner. She set her jaw defiantly and told the insufferably grinning creature, "You agreed to hire on as my investigator, which implies that you will report *everything* to me, not keep me in the dark as though I were a petulant child!"

Back to square one, thought the major. Was there no reasoning with females? "I agreed to manage the smartening up of a historic building," he retorted stiffly. "The other suggestion—the investigation of the ambush—is quite beyond your province, as it is beyond mine. What part could you hope to play in such work? I thought we had settled it that the proper agencies were already dealing with the crime?" He took a deep breath. "Now, do you wish me to assist you with the Hassleton project, or do you not? If not, I shall return to my own—employment, from which I had requested a leave of absence in order to help you."

So much for friendlier relations, mourned the girl. He has, in effect, put me in my place. I may pretend that I am his employer, but as a matter of fact he is offering me only as much of his time and attention as he wishes, to be spent in the sort of work he will agree to do! Beyond her annoyance at his male intransigence there lurked a painful sense of loss. For a few minutes it had seemed as though there was a meeting of minds, of hearts, which had been cemented by laughter. Sighing, Moira admitted that it was she who had broken the moment with her petulant demand to control Sly's behavior. She squared her shoulders and accepted the rebuff.

"You are right again. I have been difficult and ungrateful, Mr. Sly," she said quietly. "If you will forgive me, I shall be most grateful for whatever help you wish to provide."

Sly cautioned himself to stay on guard this time. It seemed that working with this little woman was like riding on a teeter-totter, swept joyously up and then jolted disconcertingly down in response to her unpredictable whims. He made his voice very cool as he replied, "Since I am no architect, nor even an expert in cleaning and restoring old buildings, my first business will be to employ knowledgeable workmen. It would never do to replace some authentic, if worm-eaten, medieval woolsack with a Georgian fakery."

"What on earth is a woolsack?" demanded Moira, unhappy at Sly's cool response to her humble, heartfelt apology. But she had lost her advantage. Sly was armored against her appeals. As she learned immediately.

"One thing more," he was telling her in a tone his subalterns would immediately have recognized. "You had better begin to call me by my proper name, since we shall be dealing with city officers and others to whom pseudonyms might appear questionable. I am Major Hilary Norman, Grenadier Guards, at present seconded to—to a member of our government who must remain nameless. You may address me as Major Norman, Miss Lovelace."

Pausing for a moment to observe the effect of this rebuke, Sly continued less harshly, "I shall get matters going at the guildhall and report to you and Mrs. Hassleton here as the need arises. I believe I have your directions for the refurbishing, and your statement as to the amount of money that may be spent."

With a smart, formal salute the major strode out of the room.

Now I've done it, the girl groaned. I've really hurt his feelings!

She discovered that this was of more concern to her than she might have expected. After all, she was not bound or committed to the soldier in any way but a business one. Why then did she feel this sense of loss, of having thrown away something very important? At least the major had agreed to return and report on the progress of the guildhall repairs. She would see him again . . . and perhaps find a way to soothe his wounded feelings.

Thoroughly convinced of her own lack of skill in dealing with men of the world, and especially with good-looking, arrogant ones, be they soldiers or noblemen, Moira spent the next half hour berating herself for her ineptitude and wondering how she could get a note of apology off to a gentleman whose address she did not know, although she had spent a night in his bedroom. Oh, of course, Pomfret would have it! He had sent the footman to summon Sly today.

Then she wasted further time thinking about her real concern, the safety of the marquess of Donat, about which she could do nothing, and trying to comfort herself with her favorite fantasy, which was to picture his beautiful violet eyes warmly admiring, his smile tender, as he bent his magnificent shoulders above her.

Only to discover that a pair of hard, challenging, yet reproachful gray eyes kept replacing the dazzling orbs of Adonis, as though reminding her who was her friend, and who her enemy. Moira had a horrid thought. Was she fickle? She had never felt a romantic interest in any man before. There had been no possible candidates in South Littlefield. And now—two men! She decided she was too vulnerable, and would have to harden her heart, put up a shield! Was that what was meant by "getting a little town bronze"? She must ask Lili.

Major Hilary Norman spent an even longer time that day cursing his own heavy-handedness in dealing with the exasperating little female. Of course, it had been *her own fault*, but, quite illogically, he found he couldn't continue to be angry with her. He was too busy being angry at himself for a cowhanded bungler.

CHAPTER FOURTEEN

The Marquess of Donat sat at the desk in his book-room, preparing himself to storm the fortress of the Lovelace woman. A rakish black-silk patch covered the healing wound on his forehead, striking a rather effective note against his golden curls. His eyebrows were drawn into a frown as he glanced through the grubby notes supplied by Nims.

Spinster.

Small wonder! The marquess's elegant nostrils flared scornfully as he rejected a fugitive memory of large, truly beautiful eyes.

Orphan. Granddaughter of a chef. Daughter of a penniless scholar. Twenty-four-years old.

She's older than I am, Adam, who was twenty-three, thought complacently. An ape-leader, in fact! It did not bother him that the difference in their ages was just a year. Any woman of twenty-four, unless she was an acknowledged beauty or a leader of society, was definitely on the shelf. For the dozenth time dismissing a disturbing memory of soft, warm flesh beneath his cheek and firmly supporting arms—for *that* must surely have been a hallucination born of the fever from his wounds or the knock on his head—Adam returned to Nims's report.

Presently living in the house of city merchant Henry Hassleton, Queen's Square. Treated as family, not servant. While still in mourning for parents, subject is not in seclusion. Is working with "Sly" to clean up guildhall for a subscription dinner. It is widely rumored that Hassleton is trying to get himself elected lord mayor!!

This last tidbit of gossip was heavily underlined. It seemed clear to Adam that his intelligencer wished him to note it carefully. Now, why—? Ah, yes! If the jumped-up cit had political ambitions, then it followed that a threat to disclose his *protégée's* criminal activities would have a powerful effect. Good! Tossing the report into a drawer, Adam rose from his desk and strode over to the window, which overlooked the square.

He had at first intended to summon the treacherous female to Donat Town House, there to confront her with his knowledge of her criminal activities and demand the name of her employer. However, Nims's research had not turned up any connection with any sort of previous activity in London. It was plain to the meanest intelligence that the chit was a new recruit to crime. Which meant, of course, that she had been enlisted by the man Sly, about whom Nims had been able to dig out absolutely nothing.

That in itself was a puzzle. Whatever Nims's background, he obviously had the knack of ferreting out even the most carefully guarded secrets. Yet he had acknowledged himself at a standstill in his investigation of Sly. Adam rubbed his chin. Could he force Lovelace to expose her fellow rogue? Certainly not if he gave her time to consult with the fellow and work up a story! Much wiser to drop in upon the woman where she lurked in the false security of the cit's home, surprise her, and under threat of ruining her host's chances at civic recognition, get the truth out of her.

Nodding decisively, the marquess strode out to the noble entrance hall—famous for its white marble floor and carved marble busts set in recesses after the Italian fashion—and demanded a closed carriage be brought around immediately. Better to give the plotters no warning of his approach!

Luck was with him. He arrived at Queen's Square at a moment when the culprit was particularly vulnerable.

Cousin Lili had rushed out at the urgent request of her modiste to settle the problem of a questionable décolletage on a gown ordered for the crucial dinner party that very night. (Was it, fretted Camille, low enough?) Henry was at his office as usual, and the servants were in a fury of activity preparing the mansion for the night's festivities. So Moira was quite alone when a young footman, substituting for Pomfret, who was engaged in the important business of making selections from the wine cellar for the dinner, announced a Mr. Sly, "about the guildhall, miss."

Moira, who was feeling lonely and dispirited, jumped up and moved eagerly forward to welcome her major—only to stop short as she saw the magnificent figure who was advancing grimly toward her from the doorway. Getting the full shock of Adonis's superb and beautiful masculinity, Moira was irresistibly put in mind of Squire Brackett's peacock, with all its colorful plumage flaunted in militant display to quell a rival.

In a panic, she tried to call back the footman to defend her against the obviously hostile nobleman. But the youth, uneasy at his unaccustomed task, had already closed the door, cutting off escape.

The marquess did not halt his menacing advance until he was within a foot of his victim. So close, in fact, was he, that the girl could catch the familiar scent of spice that clung so elegantly about Milord's person, and see the cold glare of anger in his eyes. For one long, dazzled moment, Moira was unable to tear her gaze away from the beautiful face, now thankfully healed of all but a few of the knife wounds: the sensuous mouth, the arrogant nose, the violet eyes, all crowned by a cap of golden curls. *Adonis!*

Her visitor was not similarly struck speechless. "Miss Lovelace, I presume?" he inquired.

It was most unfair to the female sex, Moira thought, that his voice should match the rest of him in masculine appeal. *Like rough black velvet.* . . . Her visitor stood waiting, a distinct sneer on his handsome countenance. Waiting—? wondered the girl. *Oh!* She gathered her scattered wits.

"Yes, I am Moira Lovelace, my lord," she managed.

108

Then, raising her glance to the rakish black patch under the golden curls, she said softly, "I am so glad you are nearly recovered!"

"No thanks to you and your fancy man," said the marquess with calculated crudeness. He had decided upon his plan of attack and was already enjoying it even more than he had expected. His eyes in their turn scanned the softly rounded female figure before him, caught momentarily by the firm globes tastefully draped by what his experience told him was a very modish and expensive black silk dress. He *knew* the way that warm, sweet-scented flesh would feel under his cheek! So she *had* held him in the carriage that night!

Suddenly the faintest quirk of doubt tugged at his mind; surely so well-dressed a young woman, treated as a member of the family in this tasteless but obviously costly mansion, would not need to hire out to a band of murderous ruffians? Her gentle consideration for his person did not match with the vicious behavior of her fellow conspirators. Perhaps she had been gulled—? Milord, feeling unusually magnanimous, opened his mouth to offer her a temporary truce—in return for everything she knew about the ambush.

He was too late.

Country mouse Moira had finally caught the reference to her "fancy man" and was furious. The marquess was proving himself as cruel and unjust as Sly had warned her he was; and she, foolishly accepting the counsel of her heart, had refused to believe it. She glared up into the amethyst eyes.

"Fancy man! That is a vile canard! It is just as everyone warned me: You are nothing but an insensitive, arrogant, pigheaded monster! So puffed-up with your own consequence and the obsequious flattery of—of sycophantic females that you cannot see truth when it hits you in the face! As I should like to do!" the little fury concluded.

Shocked by this unexpected—and unexpectedly literate—harangue, Adam had the bad taste to laugh.

Gasping with outrage, Moira took a step forward and lifted her small hand to slap her tormentor. Adam, piqued by the closer proximity of those soft globes he remembered, steeled himself to accept the blow without flinching.

To the surprise of both antagonists, Moira, after a long stare, lowered her arm to her side.

"Do hit me," invited Adam silkily. "You will feel so much better, and I shall be confirmed in my opinion of you as a vicious slut."

Moira responded quietly. "You know I cannot slap your face, no matter how much you deserve it. I might hurt your head."

"That consideration would stop you?" Adam's smile goaded her. "Don't try to gammon me, woman!"

Moira held grimly to her composure. "Why have you come here?" she asked, ignoring both his crudity and his mockery.

"To see you, of course, and discover if your bosom was as comfortable as I remembered it," sneered the nobleman. Then, meeting the steady gaze of those large brown eyes, he had the grace to say honestly, "I came to give you a last chance to tell me the truth about your part in the attack on me. If you are willing to confess all, especially the name of the person who employed you, I shall, in turn, be willing to conceal your part in the ambush—thus avoiding a scandal that would ruin Hassleton's chance to be elected lord mayor."

Moira stared at the beautiful devil in horror. He could not mean the things he had just said, the threat he had made! But perhaps Hilary and all the others who had warned her against this man were correct. Perhaps Lord Donat was in truth the self-centered monster he had been named.

At this moment something deep in Moira's being, some hitherto-untested strength, came to her assistance. Instead of railing against the false accusations, or pleading for mercy for her cousin's husband, Moira motioned her self-invited guest to a comfortable chair.

"Will you please be seated, sir? May I offer you tea?"

"What sort of game are you playing now?" snapped the

110

marquess. "*Tea?* With a woman who tried to have me murdered?"

"You have made up your mind as to my guilt in the matter, then," stated Moira as calmly as she was able. "I understood you to say you came here to learn the *truth*."

Adam seated himself in the chair with ostentatious impatience. "I take it you have decided to offer me information, then?" He gestured with one hand. "Go on."

In the same calm voice Moira recounted the events of the day leading up to the discovery of the ambush. She had scarcely got to the point of describing how she had jumped down from the coach, when the marquess sat forward angrily.

"Why do you waste my time like this?" he snapped. "I know you were working for the man Sly—"

"Mr. Sly was one of the passengers in the stagecoach," Moira continued doggedly. "When I insisted upon getting down to help you after that brute had knocked you senseless, the clergyman and Mr. Sly got down also. I asked, but no one would accompany you in your carriage to guard your head from further injury. You were unconscious; your coachman had been killed; your single groom was needed to drive the vehicle! I could not bear that any injured man should be thrown into a carriage with a dead man, to be jostled about for three hours!" Against her will, two tears overflowed her lids and slid down cheeks.

Adam tried to sneer, but there was some quality in the solemn little face across from him that prevented him. After a moment he said, "And how did *Mr. Sly* enter the picture, if you two had never met?"

"When the clergyman told me your own servants would take care of you, that it was none of my business to interfere, I—I became angry at him. I told him *someone* must play the Good Samaritan. At which point Mr. Sly laughed and came forward," she recalled meticulously. "I asked him if he would be willing to accompany me in your coach, to see you safely home. He said it was a sensible plan— and that your family would be *grateful*!" With a minatory

111

glance, she went on, "Mr. Sly agreed to help. And that is the sum of it, milord," she ended bravely.

"Not quite," Adam advised her, a little irked at the criticism of his manners implied by her emphasis on *grateful*. "There are still two matters that must be explained. The first, that you called me—a stranger whom you claim you had never heard of before—by a name used only by my intimates."

Adam paused to observe with interest the betraying color that was flooding the girl's face. The little female was *blushing*! She spoke hurriedly, her eyes for the first time failing to meet his.

"Your spies may have told you that my father was a scholar, sir? He often shared his interest and knowledge with me . . . Greek and Roman mythology. . . . When I saw your face for the first time, I—I was put in mind of Apollo—and Adonis!" Her head came up, and she faced his complacent grin proudly. "It is surely no surprise to your lordship that your—ah—countenance should remind anyone of those two mythical figures? After all, your *friends* have all made the connection!"

Finding himself to be pleased rather than affronted by this frank declaration, the marquess compelled himself to return to the second point at issue.

"Thank you for the compliment," he said in a tone he tried to make mocking. "There is, I am afraid, another question I must ask. How is it that you came to deal so well with this *chance-met* acquaintance, Sly, that you agreed to spend the night with him? Did he, too, remind you of one of the Greek gods? I am given to understand that you did not present yourself at this house until the following morning."

Moira's face was again flaunting its colors, but this time the emotion behind the blush was fury at the insult. How fortunate that she had not betrayed Major Norman's identity to this monster! "What excellent spies you have, my lord! I am sure it would be no use at all to tell you I was so exhausted from holding your not-inconsiderable bulk in my arms for three hours—at the end, I might add, of a day

112

crowded with bruising accidents in the stagecoach—that I could hardly hold my head erect by the time we delivered you to your house. Having assured ourselves that you were in competent hands, with a physician in attendance, we went out to the carriage—*your carriage*, milord, which your splendid groom, moved by a sense of gratitude apparently rare in your household, had arranged to send us to our own homes in.'' The little virago, breathless from her harangue, favored her inquisitor with a jaundiced glare. For some reason the marquess found this amusing.

Fuming, Moira continued. ''At this time I discovered that, since it was well after midnight, I might find it awkward to sign into a hostel in a strange city. At which point the man who had so graciously assisted me in *rescuing you* offered me the courtesy of his home for the rest of the night. I could hardly have forced myself upon my cousin's kindness at that hour!''

Adam was experiencing two emotions hitherto rare to him: a sense of embarrassment at his own failure to express suitable gratitude for the young woman's efforts on his behalf, which had been truly commendable in a stranger, and a rampant curiosity to know exactly what had been the nature and extent of the *hospitality* offered by the man Sly. Adam searched the woman's face boldly, trying to solve the mystery she was presenting to him. Steady brown eyes met his fearlessly, challenging his manhood—and his courtesy.

Since he had never had to apologize to any living creature in his life, he found it difficult to do so to this knaggy little spinster. Still—noblesse oblige! Squaring his shoulders, he said stiffly, ''Much obliged to you, Miss Lovelace, for your trouble in seeing me safe home. I had thought—mistakenly, I am beginning to believe—that you were in league with the conspirators. You must admit the evidence was against you—''

At this point, he became aware that his proposed apology and thanks were taking more the form of another accusation. If he had not noticed it himself, he would certainly

113

have been made conscious of his ineptitude by the growing flush of annoyance on the girl's face.

Moira raised her hand as arrogantly as the marquess had ever done. "Enough, milord! You bog yourself down deeper with every carping word! Let us cry quits. I freely release you from any further need to apologize or feel gratitude. You, for your part, may control your rampant imagination to the extent of accepting my innocence of any wish to harm you—or, in fact, *ever to set eyes on you again!*"

Well! That was definite enough, acknowledged the marquess. He had never in all his spoiled life been addressed with quite such stern criticism, such open dislike. He was willing to admit that he had handled the affair of the compassionate spinster with less than his usual aplomb. Damn it, he wasn't sure why his normal skill at manipulating his fellow humans had failed so badly with this little nobody. In fact, it appeared he had bungled the matter so thoroughly that he would never be permitted to see the woman again.

At that thought he paused. Never see her again? But surely that was a consummation devoutly to be desired, was it not? His *goal*, if she had proved innocent of the charges. If she was not guilty—and that had been the consensus of all his advisers except Nims—there was no need to meet with her again.

Then, why did he have the feeling that he had just lost an important contest? He told himself it was time he made his adieus, got himself out of the merchant's pretentious mansion before the little shrew had him evicted.

Moira shocked him again.

Her conscience had been hurting her over the much-needed setdown she had been forced to give the arrogant nobleman. Some illogical urge to prolong the conversation prompted her to babble, "I suppose I must warn you that I hired Mr. Sly to investigate the ambush, with the hope of discovering the culprits and protecting you from another vicious attack . . ." Moira hesitated, alarmed by the flush of outrage the marquess was exhibiting. ". . . and to free myself from further false charges," she ended hastily.

"Indeed?" grated the nobleman. "So I am to understand

that *Miss Lovelace* is now to assume the role of my protector, guardian, *wet nurse*?'' Adam raged on, delighted with the chance to give the impudent female some of her own medicine. ''I am to have my privacy invaded and my peace shattered by a motley crew of commoners, prying and meddling into my affairs? *I think not*, Miss Interfering Lovelace!''

Moira had originally intended to go on, chattily, to reveal the true name and style of Hilary Norman. The ugly attack by the marquess changed her mind.

''My only thought was to protect *my* privacy, and *my* good name, from your wicked calumnies!'' she lied. His remark about a wet nurse had made her almost as furious as he appeared to be. ''I am not at all sure how far one may safely trust the *noble marquess*'s clemency, since his perception of *facts* changes from moment to moment!''

By now anxious to get himself away from the chit before he did her an injury, the marquess treated her to his most elaborate bow, to a tight-lipped, humorless smile, and to the sight of his splendid shoulders vanishing through the doorway.

Moira sank into a chair and sat staring in front of her at a particularly ugly portrait of Henry Hassleton until Cousin Lili came in search of her, with orders to dress immediately or she would be late for the dinner in her own honor.

CHAPTER FIFTEEN

Cousin Lili bustled into Moira's bedroom that evening to check on her protégée's appearance. She stopped short in real surprise as she saw what a top-of-the-trees modiste like Camille could do with a twenty-four-year-old spinster, given time, a free hand, and unlimited finances. Lili had never really appreciated the girl's figure, clothed as it had been on arrival in a dowdy redingote, and since then in a hastily assembled, somber, ready-to-wear wardrobe.

The new garment, designed and tailored to present the young woman's figure at its feminine best, created a breathtaking effect. What excellent breasts the girl had, proudly shaped above a slender waist! And displayed to full advantage by the clinging Empire dress, thought Lili with a smothered giggle. The color, a dark amber, was more suitable for a young woman past her first blush than an insipid pastel would have been. Even more remarkable was the way the rich, soft color enhanced the girl's complexion and brought the truly beautiful brown eyes to one's notice. How was it that so downy a bird as Lili conceived herself to be had missed the unusual quality of her country cousin? *Épatant!*

Striking Moira certainly was. Where she had appeared stocky, she was now revealed to be richly yet sweetly curved. And her hair! Lili had to give credit to her own dresser, the formidable Totham, for creating a smooth, shining crown in place of the shaggy, badly cut undisciplined mass of hair the girl had sported on her arrival. The

116

color, alas, was neither dashingly brunet nor dazzlingly blond. It was a soft brown, a little lighter than her eyes. But Totham had rendered it into a silky coronet, which displayed to good advantage the high cheekbones, delicate straight nose, and generous soft mouth. To say nothing of the beautiful eyes. The girl was no diamond, Lili conceded honestly, nor was she likely to set the beau monde agog. Perhaps, given Moira's background, that was just as well. Lili planned to marry her cousin off well, but snaring a nobleman was far beyond her dreams. So now she complimented Moira most sincerely upon the striking improvement in her appearance and asked Totham whether she should not apply a little of the marvelous maquillage Camille had supplied. She was surprised when both the other women chuckled.

"Told you she wouldn't spot it," crowed Totham, with a good humor strikingly at odds with her normal gloom.

"Totham *has* applied color to my cheeks, and just a breath of it to my lips," confessed Moira. "I was afraid it would make me look silly—but you can't even detect it!"

"Then, why bother?" snapped the Frenchwoman, peering crossly into the dressing-table mirror at her own well-painted face.

Her testy mood did not last, however; she was too pleased with the effect a little savoir faire could create.

Even Henry, impatiently waiting in the drawing room for the ladies to arrive, was impressed by the picture they made as they entered the large, ostentatiously furnished apartment.

"You took so long over your dressing, I thought I should have to greet our guests by myself," he grumbled. Then his heavy features softened into a smile. "It was worth it," he conceded. "You both look as fine as fivepence!"

Whatever Lili might have replied to this very mundane compliment was not known, for Pomfret threw open the double doors at this moment to announce the first of the guests.

Within the next twenty minutes, Henry was pleased to behold every single person who had received an invitation to meet his wife's cousin entering his drawing room. Most of the guests were Henry's fellow merchants and their wives. One or two had adult offspring especially invited as companions for Miss Lovelace. One alderman and his wife had accepted the invitation. And a doubtful Henry had acceded to Lili's insistence, permitting her to include Mr. Sly on the list.

"But none of us *knows* the fellow!" the merchant had protested. "Chance-met on a stagecoach! He could be *anybody*! And with a name like that—!"

"He brought Moira safely to us," Lili reminded him. "And helped her rescue the wounded nobleman."

"A fat lot of gratitude the nobleman showed," grumbled Henry. "Not even a posy or a note of thanks!"

"He did pay a duty call today," ventured Moira.

Mr. Hassleton's eyebrows lifted. "Someone might have told me," he sniffed. It occurred to him that a connection with one of London's elite might in some way be brought to his advantage. Filing that idea for later consideration, Henry waited with mounting suspicion for the arrival of the fellow with the queer name.

Moira was having second thoughts as the minutes ticked by. She should have warned Cousin Lili about Sly's real name and position; but she was not sure under which guise he would choose to present himself. She should have asked Hilary not to accept the invitation, but she still had no idea of his address. Had Lili invited him the last time he had called, or had she obtained his address through Pomfret? Of course, her worldly-wise cousin had been ignorant of the quarrel and the succeeding coldness between her cousin and the *executive officer*, as he had so charmingly designated himself. Moira had not heard from him, or of him, since that disastrous interview in the ladies' parlor, when they had swung between warm accord and chilling anger. Unfortunately, they had parted upon the latter note, and Moira had a lowering conviction that the gallant soldier would send his excuses rather than meet again with so ungrateful a female as herself.

The officer made his appearance just as Lili was getting

ready to give the signal to enter the dining room. When Pomfret announced Major Hilary Norman, there was so much satisfaction in the butler's voice that the eyes of nearly everyone in the room swiveled to the doorway to take in the restrained magnificence of the newcomer's dress uniform, and the even more impressive self-confidence in the handsome officer's expression and bearing.

It was fortunate that the guests were looking at the soldier rather than at their hosts, for the same ludicrous expression of shock decorated each of the three faces. Henry, who had never met Mr. Hilary Sly, and who had been, moreover, given a carefully edited account of the rescue on the stagecoach, was wondering if this top-o'-the-trees military man had gotten himself into the wrong party. Then, as the name Hilary rang a bell—for Henry was no fool—a horrid suspicion that Lili had togged out the ex-soldier in a rented costume to puff off his (nonexistent) consequence turned the host's welcoming smile into an angry glare.

Lili, quicker to the mark than her husband, defused the potentially explosive situation by taking the arm of the most distinguished guest, the city alderman who had consented to grace their party, and announcing in a clear voice, "Shall we go in to dinner, ladies and gentlemen?"

As Henry, reminded of his duty, sought out the alderman's wife to offer his arm, Moira warily watched the enigmatic major advance toward her. The officer stood out among the overdressed self-consequential group of cits like an eagle among barnyard fowls. Or, Moira warned herself, catching the steely glint in those gray eyes, like a wolf in a flock of fat sheep!

As the wolf loomed over her, offering his arm in correct form, Moira scanned the dark face. The silver eyes were narrowed with amusement, she was relieved to observe. His thin upper lip cut a straight line across the white teeth. The lower lip, she noted, was sensuously full and curved above a strong chin. He had the most distracting smile she had ever seen.

"Impressed?" asked the man, with far too much awareness of the effect he was creating.

In spite of her surprise at the metamorphosis of Sly into Major Hilary Norman, Moira found herself enjoying this encounter very much indeed. *He had forgiven her!* Ignoring the effect the dashing soldier was having upon her emotions, Moira took the offered arm. She smiled delightfully up into the dark, admiring face. Two could play at this game, she discovered with pleasure. She had a new rig-out, too!

"Impressed?" she tossed back naughtily.

"May I be permitted to tell you how charming you look this evening, Miss Lovelace?" asked the deep voice.

"You may," smiled Moira. "In fact, you probably *have to*, whatever you actually think!" She grinned like an urchin. "I only hope you can carry off this—ah—masquerade without involving us all in a scandal."

"Brat," retorted the soldier appreciatively. "Shall we follow our host, who is most correctly following his wife, who is most correctly leading the way with the guest of honor—which you, actually, should most correctly be, but are not?"

Moira chuckled, recalling just this silly wordplay from their very first meeting. She permitted the soldier to escort her into the dining room, where the guests were already taking their places around the massive table. Sly, seating her near the middle of one side, let his glance slide over the much-too-elaborate furnishings.

"Don't say it!" warned the girl, eyes twinkling. "Don't even think it! Your position here among the cits is untenable, Major; unprotected, solitary, and vulnerable!"

"On the contrary, Miss L," announced the gallant officer with smug complacence, "I am known as the Hostess's Dream. I am handsome, of good style and impeccable lineage, dazzling in my dress uniform. The perfect partner, in fact, for a middle-aged spinster-relative up from the country." Then, grinning, the wretch waited for the caustic setdown they both knew the girl could not permit herself to make in this situation.

Moira surprised him. With an affected titter, she rolled her lovely eyes at him, and said, in a voice clearly audible to their neighbors on either side, "La, Major Norman! Such a *charming* compliment, but quite untrue! I vow I cannot accept such brummagem!"

Observing the voracious, poorly concealed interest in everyone within reach of her clear voice, the major surrendered and seated his little battlemaid without further badinage. As he took his place beside her, his grin made that devastating white slash in his brown face.

"Every good soldier enjoys a challenge," he told her softly. "That is a precept one learns at one's sergeant's—ah—knee." Then he offered quite a different smile to her wary brown gaze. Tender. Supportive. "Be at ease, child! I really am a major, as I told you when last we met—was it only this afternoon?—my name is Norman, and I have truly come to help, not to hinder. Since I am sure to meet some of these merchants during the refurbishing of the guildhall, I could not risk getting us into an imbroglio with a pseudonym like Sly."

"Obviously a nickname given you by your fellow officers," teased the girl softly. "And well-deserved, I should think!" Then, before he could reply to that thrust, Moira went on, "Have you anything to report to me, Executive Officer?"

She was expecting a few words concerning Sly's progress at the guildhall. The major surprised her.

"Quite a bit, but it had better wait until a less public moment, I think. It involves a spy set to watch you by the Marquess of Donat."

Moira was forced to concede, with a sinking feeling, that spies and vengeful noblemen were hardly the most desirable material for discussion at a formal dinner party. The comment also reminded her of Sly's announcement that he had asked Bow Street to detail a Runner to protect her. Though she strove to hide the emotions, both alarm and annoyance were reflected in Moira's expressive little countenance.

The major could have done himself an injury for so crassly intruding serious business into a social occasion. I have been too long at war, he chastised himself. In the hope of retrieving the situation, he set himself to charm and interest his neighbors at the table. Their awe of the resplendent military uniform was soon overcome. Sly made some flattering references to the wonderful assistance the people of London had given their armies overseas, and their support of Wellington against his niggling detractors at home, and the ice was broken. Then the wily Major welcomed questions as to his own connection with the brightening up of the guildhall. He was able to toss in some admiring comments on the historical importance of the government of the city by its lord mayor, sheriffs, and aldermen, which service went back—"as I have no need to remind *this* company!"—to William the Conqueror's treaty with the city in 1066.

Catching and holding the dazzled stares, Sly added, "At that time they, under their city leader or *alderman*," with an inclination toward the honor-guest, "fought bravely. Their alderman was wounded, but they *wouldn't give up*!"

This was well-received.

Next he reminded his audience, which consisted by now of every person at the large table, of the history of the guildhall, its dreadful destruction in the Great Fire of 1666, and its splendid rebuilding.

Henry was heard to repeat, *"They wouldn't give up!"*

Alderman Frizzel proposed a toast to that sentiment, which was duly honored.

Then Sly spoke warmly of the splendid example the guildhall presented of government-by-the-people—the freemen, merchants, guildsmen all working sensibly and effectively together to insure fair and equitable treatment for all the citizens of the city of London. By the time dinner was over, the guests were vociferously expressing the opinion that this had been the best and most interesting function they had attended in a long time. And when, flushed with Henry's excellent wine, the alderman proposed a toast to "Our gracious host, Mr. Hassleton, who has given so generously to restore the luster of our beloved guildhall!" it was honored with a right goodwill by everyone present.

The sense of well-deserved pride continued throughout

the evening. When the last guest finally departed (it was Major Norman), Henry wrung his hand warmly.

Rejoining the weary ladies in the drawing room, Henry was almost speechless with satisfaction. Almost. He first thanked Pomfret, who had been responsible for the inspired selection of wines and liqueurs to accompany the food, as well as for the smooth running of the entire function. Then he smiled at Lili, enjoying her pert response. Finally he turned his sharp gaze upon Moira, who was beaming happily at her cousin.

"Thank you, Cousin Lili, for my welcome party!" she said.

Henry gave an approving nod. "You did well, Moira. Oh, I know you've been behind my Lili, cheering her along, acting the dogsbody! But the best thing you ever did was to hire that soldier fellow to carry out my orders for cleaning the hall." He shook his head admiringly. "He sold it to 'em, from A to Izzard, and he sold *me* to 'em as well! Alderman Frizzel and that wife of his will have it all through the wards before breakfast tomorrow! What was it you said, girl? The name of Henry Hassleton, forever linked to the guildhall!" He rubbed his hands together delightedly. "It's true, by George!"

Buoyed up by the general euphoria, Moira dared to hope that her host was correct, and that all her troubles were over. Unfortunately she had forgotten Sly's ominous information about the marquess's spy, and did not recall it until she was lying in bed, drowsily reviewing the satisfying events of the evening. When she did remember, her body stiffened. It seemed that Adonis still distrusted her—hated her. There was always the possibility that Sly's intelligence was dated, that the marquess had dismissed his spy after the stormy encounter in Lili's parlor. Surely Milord was convinced of her innocence now?

The girl lay awake for a long time, remembering the feeling of a head covered with golden curls pressed against her breast.

CHAPTER SIXTEEN

Adam waited impatiently for his intelligencer the following morning. Nims was usually well before time, sitting silently in the servants' hall fingering his grubby notebook. But today he did not appear. The marquess finally came out of his library to look for him and was told that the fellow hadn't shown his face that day.

A groom was immediately dispatched to Nims's lodgings, where it was learned that Nims had not been seen for two days, although he had been visited by one or two men, and had been heard by the manager to leave with one of them late at night.

Adam tried to remember exactly what new information he had sent Nims to ferret out. He had been ordered to track down the fellow Sly, of course, and to discover what he could about Vivian Donat's scurrilous attacks upon Adam's reputation. Nims had offered to try to find out what the latest scandalous bit of gossip was concerned with, and if possible, *who* was helping Vivian to spread the filth.

It was not hard to spread rumors in the hotbed of London society. A word dropped here, a knowing smile there, an *on-dit* whispered into an avid ear, and the thing was done. A man's or a woman's reputation blasted, families humiliated, ancient names debased. Adam was brooding over the idea that Vivian seemed to have little respect for the name and consequence that, after all, were as much his as Adam's, when he was interrupted by his butler announcing a messenger from the magistrate's office at Bow Street.

The Runner correctly remained at attention as he delivered his message. The body of one Alfred Nims (age unknown; profession unknown; address, a grimy mews in a back alley of the city of London) had been discovered by the indignant head clerk of Weston's, tailor to the ton, on old Bond Street this morning, just outside the doorway of the establishment. Said body now waiting at the morgue for positive identification by Milord the marquess.

Adam was thunderstruck. "But how did you connect the man Nims with me—?" he stammered, with some idea of denying any knowledge. "If Vivian has made some absurd statement—"

"We are not at liberty to reveal our sources, milord."

Adam's frown would have made a weaker man quail. "What business could this possibly be of mine?" he demanded.

"A note was found in the pocket of the deceased, milord." The Runner took his neat commonplace-book from his pocket, thumbed pages until he reached his goal, and then read in a carefully unemotional voice:

"I beg your lordship will give me a chance to explain this matter. I have not shared your secret with anyone, I swear it! I have done exactly as you ordered me. Your lordship should know that I would never betray you, whatever the temptation offered."

The Runner closed his record book and stared hard at the stunned nobleman as he concluded, "The note was signed Alfred Nims, milord, and was addressed on the cover to you."

Such is the quiet efficiency of the Runners that Adam found himself in his own carriage, driving with the officer down to Bow Street, without quite realizing how it was happening. There followed a daunting half hour spent viewing the body and denying that he had written—or even seen—the note in evidence. Then the marquess was permitted to leave. The magistrate's final words were a suggestion that Milord might wish to discuss this situation with

Mr. Beresford . . . and a request for a sample of his handwriting.

In no time at all the news was around London's beau monde. Some wretched spy was dead, and, rumor had it, his killer was the Marquess of Donat. Opinion in the clubs was pretty sharply divided.

Sir Will Fotriss was loud in his belief that that damned fop Donat had gone too far this time. "I hope they hang 'im!''

Lord Rundle, a neighbor of Adam's, rejected that point of view, and gave it as *his* considered opinion that one of Donat's former dueling adversaries was avenging a painful loss on the field of honor by means of a theatrical crime.

"For it stands to reason," Lord Rundle argued, "that any man wishing to be rid of an embarrassment would hardly leave a note directed to himself in the fellow's pocket. Adonis is not *that* stupid."

To which there was general, if reluctant, agreement.

Sly himself brought the word to Moira the following morning. He had known of the discovery of the body soon after Bow Street heard of it, and he had spent a long night trying to decide how much—if anything—to tell the girl. For, of course, little mother-hen that she was, she would fly to the nobleman's defense! Sly knew she was bound to hear of the matter shortly, gossip being what it was. Still, the soldier feared Moira's excitable, strongly partisan nature. He would not soon forget the fiercely resolute little air with which Miss Lovelace had taken over the protection and succor of the wounded marquess. And anyone who cared a fig for Miss Lovelace's standing in the ton must warn her not to thrust herself headlong into so dangerous a matter as the scandal that was brewing over the murder of the spy.

With a groan part frustration, part affection, the soldier accepted his burden. Within ten minutes he had set out for the Hasselton mansion. He was welcomed by Pomfret, who had, of course, heard of the brouhaha, and respectfully ushered this loyal supporter of Miss Lovelace into her presence.

"She hasn't heard yet," Pomfret managed to mutter. Then, greatly daring, he pleaded, "You won't let Miss get tangled up in the business, will you, Major Norman?"

Sly shared a rueful glance with the butler. "I shall do my best," he promised, and was rewarded by a grateful bow.

Moira rose happily and came forward to greet Hilary.

"Well, this is pleasant, I must say!" she told him. "Your duty call so early?" She cast a sly glance at his empty hands and teased, "What, no posy? A glaring oversight, Major!"

The soldier was loath to break such a charming mood. For one treacherous moment, he considered just basking in the sweetness of this meeting, sharing laughter with this darling female, and letting some other spoilsport give her the bad news about her nobleman.

It was then that Hilary Norman realized that he could not permit any other man to hurt the girl—or to offer the needed comfort and assistance to her. *He* was Moira's executive officer. He accepted his fate with a grim smile. *Hooked at last!*

"No, dear child, no posy this morning. We have a problem to face. A very serious one." To underline his meaning, Sly strode back, tiger-silent, to the door, and turned the latch.

Moira caught on at once. Gesturing to a position beside her, she seated herself on a small sofa and said in a quiet voice, "Bad news, Sly? How can I help?"

The soldier wasted no time. "You may recall that I mentioned a spy set to watch you by—the marquess?"

Moira nodded, her expression grave.

"His body has been found on Bond Street. In one pocket was a note addressed to Donat, containing some incriminating remarks. One theory is that the marquess killed him to avoid blackmail—or exposure."

"But you do not believe this," the girl said.

Sly was proud of her composure. What a splendid sergeant she would have made! he thought. Never flustered—or very seldom (he remembered a *few* flares of anger)—quick to assess a situation! He nodded.

"I cannot believe so downy a bird as our Adonis would allow himself to be so badly betrayed by emotion," he said, trying to lighten the discussion. "He would far more likely have paid the blackmailer and torn up the note."

Moira was frowning. Considering her experience with the arrogant nobleman, her opinion was that he might well have knocked the man down and taken the note. She remembered the sight of that battered, blood-spattered figure lunging and thrusting and kicking against his attackers on the shadowy highroad. Still, she must accept the soldier's judgment as both honest and possibly more knowledgeable than her own.

"Was there anything more?" she asked, reading his expression.

The soldier nodded approval of her perceptivity. "Yes, actually. A very strange little quirk. Nims's coat was turned inside out."

"Turncoat?" mused the girl.

She *was* quick! Sly thought admiringly. The problem of the turned coat had teased at him. He could not visualize the elegant marquess acting as valet for the dingy Nims, alive or dead. He shared this insight.

Moira nodded. "You know, Sly, this whole thing isn't like Adam Donat. A murder in an alley, changing a dirty coat on a dead body, leaving betraying clues—! It's stupid!"

Sly's quizzical expression brought a quick response.

"Of course, Adon—Adam Donat has done some things you and I might label less than well-considered." She managed to ignore the man's nod of hearty agreement. "It seems to me that this is a scheme to incriminate the marquess. And we know there are several people whose enmity is great enough to wish him dead."

"I believe that Magistrate Rowley shares your opinion. Otherwise we should already have Milord in gaol," said the major.

128

And then came the offer he was dreading.

"Major Norman," the girl said solemnly, "we must both enlist our brains to discover the true culprit. It is our duty!"

"As long as it's only your *brain* you enlist, I shall gladly accept the assignment," said the major formally and firmly. "The furbishing-up of the guildhall is in the capable hands of several guilds, each skilled at its own craft. My—superior officer has reluctantly given me a leave of absence to continue to help you until the dinner is successfully brought off. I shall, *upon one condition*, also set myself to solving the mystery of the turned coat." And then, realizing from her expression that his companion was not amused by his levity, he finished quietly, "I shall do my best to discover the real murderer of Alfred Nims."

Moira's smile expressed her deep gratitude for this handsome offer. Leaning toward him in the close confines of the little love seat, she grasped his big hard hand in both of hers and carried it close to her breast in a spontaneous gesture of thanks.

"Hilary!" she breathed, beaming up at the delighted fellow with glowing eyes. "How *good* you are! *Now* we shall contrive!"

As his hand pressed the softness of those adorable globes, so sweetly encased in silk, the soldier felt as though he had been struck by lightning. He could not believe that the girl's delicious response was solely caused by her admiration of the beautiful marquess. There was surely an appreciation of Sly's own skills, daring, and willingness to help her? If he did succeed in solving the problem, her attention would be focused upon a hardworking, loyal, well-set-up, and surely not-unattractive soldier, rather than on a spoiled, willful aristocrat?

Major Hilary Norman had discovered that he was ready to enter the state of matrimony, even if it meant giving up his exciting work for the prime minister. In fact, he intended to storm the citadel of one delightful little woman, and accept nothing but total surrender! So great had been the power of that soft, delicious touch! Earthshaking!

"I shall have to clear with Bow Street," Sly warned her

when he had recovered enough breath to speak. "And there is still the matter of my stipulation." He tried to sound stern and succeeded, if her expressive little countenance was any criterion for judgment, in sounding silly.

She was chuckling. "Stipulation!" she teased. "You know you have me over a barrel," she said, and then added with a naughty chuckle, "as the innkeeper's wife said to her customers."

Caught between wicked delight at the image that phrase conjured up, and the need to censure the chit's unruly tongue, the soldier surrendered with a laugh.

"Whyever am I worrying about your acquiring town bronze when you are so well-supplied with rustic rhetoric?" he demanded.

Both of them dissolved into laughter, the grim business at hand forgotten for a few precious moments.

It was a couple of days later before Sly remembered that he had never explained his "stipulation" to the girl, but he shrugged and forgot it. He'd told her often enough not to meddle!

CHAPTER SEVENTEEN

The following morning, while the ladies were talking rather solemnly over their coffee of the events of the previous day, several large boxes were delivered bearing the distinctive label of the modiste Camille. When Pomfret indulgently announced the arrival, Lili's black eyes sparkled, and she swept Moira with her up to her boudoir to examine the treasures.

"Life must continue, my dear girl, and our obligations to poor Henry's dream and the guildhall are *important*."

Fascinated by the logic of this statement, Moira joined her kind hostess, Totham, and Annie in Mrs. Hassleton's boudoir, where for two exciting hours they forgot everything in the sheer pleasure of trying on one dazzling creation after another.

"Of course you will wear *this one* to dinner at the guildhall." Lili held up the romantic gown Moira had fallen in love with when they visited the modiste's establishment. "But which should you wear tonight?" the older woman went on. "It's the rout given by Lady Benedict. She's the mother of Donat's best friend, you know. It's an invitation that can include you, Moira! 'Mr. and Mrs. Hassleton *and party*,' no less! I wonder how they knew about you?"

Moira was strongly of the opinion that Lady Benedict, whoever she was, knew nothing and cared less for one Moira Lovelace of South Littlefield. Unless—? Unless Adonis had mentioned her! Delicious warmth rose in the girl as she considered that possibility. Pulling herself together, very much aware of Cousin Lili's discerning glance, Moira replied, "However Lady Benedict heard of me, it was kind of her to invite me. I'd like to go. It will be interesting to see how the great folk go on!" The thought that a certain blond nobleman might be one of the guests kept the unusual warmth circulating in her blood.

Lili was busy ruffling through the new dresses Camille had sent for Moira. With a triumphant cry, she held up one garment of bright yellow. "Perfect with your brown hair and eyes!" she declared.

Controlling her impulse to reject the too-colorful dress out of hand, Moira said gently, "I must not forget that I am in mourning, dear Lili, and probably shouldn't be going to such a grand affair in the first place!"

"But you will come, child?" begged her cousin. "It will be such a squeeze that no one will meet anyone, really! Not so as to know *who* they are, or whether they should be languishing at home in black gloves!"

Moira did not take this plain-speaking in the wrong spirit. Lili knew how sincerely her young cousin mourned the charming Lovelaces. But both women were realists: life had to go on, and the more courageously one faced it, the better for all concerned. Herbert and Candace would have approved heartily.

"Is it a masquerade?" the girl asked hopefully. It would be diverting to attend a real ball, in the home of persons who were of the same social order as the marquess!

Lili was scanning the invitation.

"Oh!" her spirits seemed a little deflated. "Now I see why the guests are urged to bring their own party! It is a *benefit*, just as the guildhall dinner is! A subscription affair! *Donations accepted*!"

"What is Lady Benedict's charity?" Moira asked.

Lili was peering at the fine script. Muttering something about a wretched *hand*, she finally announced, "It appears to be in support of some almshouses endowed by the host's father. I haven't heard of these particular ones, but I understand that there are several privately sponsored hospices in the poorer districts of the city, and on the outskirts."

"Surely a worthy cause," suggested Moira, suddenly very eager to attend the function, mercenary though its sponsors might appear. "We can send the Benedicts an invitation to the dinner at the guildhall, and get back some of Henry's blunt that way."

Lili greeted this outrageous idea with the applause it deserved, and then turned to the more important matter of the costumes they should wear to the rout-ball.

Moira's glance had returned frequently to a romantic little dress she did not remember having seen during the visit to Camille's boutique. It was white, and had a rosy sash high under the breast, and little puffed sleeves. A charming silk ruff outlined the modest neckline. She shook her head regretfully, and said to Lili, "Of course it's too *ingénue* in style for an ape-leader like me, and the color is unsuitable with black gloves, but isn't it a *darling*?"

Lili's eyes gleamed with satisfaction at the girl's pleasure. Her voice was quiet as she remarked casually, "That's what I thought when I saw it at Camille's. I spoke to her about it, and warned her you would think it too young or too bright or too *something*. Camille had a *coup du ciel*, you would say, gift from heaven? She designed this overdress," burrowing about in the box. "She tells me it will be quite *convenable*, even for a girl who is in black gloves. Voilà!"

Lili drew out a filmy, faintly lustrous garment from the box. As she held it up, it seemed no more than a wisp of gray smoke, without definition. Moira cast a very skeptical glance at her cousin.

"I do hope, Cousin Lili, for Henry's sake at least, that you are not suggesting I make an appearance in that bit of nothing?"

Lili giggled. "Put on the pretty dress, girl, and let us see what Camille had in mind."

With much help from Totham and Annie, who were agog over the whole affair, Moira was eased into the pretty white dress. While Annie held the rosy sash, Lili shook out the lustrous gray-silver overdress. Then she and Totham pulled and twitched and tugged Camille's brainstorm over Moira's head and shoulders and down to the hem of the white dress.

And then they caught their collective breaths. The effect was completely different. Gone was the sweetly childish air the costume had formerly presented. In its place was a subtly elegant, soigné creation that fairly shouted Paris, high style—and a touch of mystery! The color now was a richly vital silver, without flash or glitter. Lacking the rosy sash, the dress was no longer an ingenue's garment but a subdued enticement, a statement of femininity.

"A wig!" pronounced Totham imperiously. "Miss Moira must wear a white wig!"

"Silver?" suggested Lili, frowning.

Totham shook her head. "Not with that sweet young face," she argued. "But the white will blend in, madam, and give just a touch of *former days*, as you might say."

"A tribute to Lady Benedict's father-in-law, who established the almshouses," proposed Moira, quite above herself with pleasure at the success of the dress on her—as she had always believed—rather prosaic person. "Didn't the nobs wear white wigs fifty years ago? Do you suppose we can find one?"

And to herself she was saying, "Adonis will see me looking like *this*!" Her heart sang.

CHAPTER EIGHTEEN

Lady Benedict's charity ball turned out to be the most dramatic social event of the Season. Any one of the several outrageous things that occurred at it would have made the rout the talk of London. When all of them were considered, it was not surprising that one social arbiter was quoted as saying that she intended to cancel her own scheduled dinner party at once, since absolutely NOTHING could ever equal, much less top, the Benedict disaster.

It all began normally enough, with far too many magnificent carriages jostling for position in the wide street in front of Benedict Town House. There, illuminated by half a hundred flambeaux, red-coated footmen ran up and down a red carpet that stretched from the road to the huge front doors, assisting elegantly clothed guests to leave their coaches and enter the mansion. By ten o'clock, it was clear that the Benedict rout was to be one of the most notable crushes of the Season. Dukes and their duchesses, marquesses and marchionesses, earls and countesses, all jostled elbows with the lord mayor, most of the aldermen and *their* wives, and a horde of lesser lights. It was confirmed that the Prince would grace the affair with his presence by eleven *post meridiem*.

Success!

And then, while the guests were crowding and pushing at the punch bowls and the various buffets, muttering rudely about nipcheese hosts and *almshouse bills of fare*, the trouble began. The beau monde's golden boy, Adam Donat, started the avalanche. He arrived late, just before Prinny was due to appear, and was, in consequence, given a rather hurried welcome by his flustered hostess. Lady Benedict had been appalled by the success of her subscription party. It had been intended as a sop to her husband's family pride. She had certainly not anticipated such an overwhelming response. Where she had invited dozens, scores came. Already her chef had run out of food and was having an explosion of Gallic temperament in the kitchen. The Prince was due to arrive at any moment, and her buffleheaded husband, Lord Lambert Benedict, had just informed his wife that he had forgotten to order the port that was His Royal Highness's favorite tipple! And now Adonis appeared—so late as to interfere with the proper reception of royalty! It was enough to make any hostess cross! Lady Benedict gave society's spoiled darling a very short shrift indeed, bustling him off with a suggestion that he go find himself something to drink.

Adonis was not accustomed to such treatment. Glaring around the enormous rooms for a glimpse of his friend John, the marquess presented a romantic if sullen figure. His only concession to his healing injury was the black silk patch high on his forehead. Aside from the fact that his head ached painfully at odd times during the day, and the equally annoying fact that he couldn't get one brown-eyed little chit out of his mind, Adam was ready to assume full control of his own life again. Find his enemies; destroy them. He was anxious to discuss this program with John. Where was the fellow?

When he could catch no sight of his best friend among all the crowds, Adam began to wonder if John's absence and Lady Benedict's cavalier treatment of an old family friend might be a foretaste of rejections to come? Of course, word of the Nims fiasco had spread throughout the ton!

Deciding that he needed the offered drink, Adam searched for a buffet. When he saw the mob surging and struggling around the tables, however, Adam's temper flared. What kind of woman gives a party and asks so many people that none of them can be comfortable? he asked

136

himself. Remembering that the only reason he himself had come was to talk with John, Adam again scanned the crowd for the tall, urbane figure.

Again, no success. He had just decided, in rather a pettish mood, to return forthwith to the comfort of his own home, when he heard an all-too-familiar voice. It was that of his cousin Vivian, and Vivian was talking about Adam.

"Of course Adam killed the fellow!" Vivian was in the process of announcing to a group of avid listeners. "My mama has always said, when one deals with scum like that ferret Nims, one is bound to get slime on oneself!"

Such a gust of rage swept Adam that it left him shaking. How dared the little weasel make such a dastardly charge against the head of his house? And quote his antidote of a mother as an authority! Adam knew that Callista and Vivian Donat hated him, but he had not considered that they might flaunt that hatred so openly in society. Not even pausing to think of the effect—for when had Adonis ever needed to consider such things?—Adam thrust his way into the center of the little group and knocked Vivian down.

There was a small oasis of shocked silence amid the general uproar of the party. Then one gentleman cried, "Bravo, Donat! Well-done!," two other gentlemen withdrew rapidly from the shameful melee, the crowd surged closer, and two ladies fainted.

Since the crush was truly overwhelming, neither of the ladies actually fell to the floor, but were draped, more or less gracefully, over persons close to them. While the unfortunate members of the group endeavored to sort out this imbroglio, Lady Benedict's butler bellowed, *"His Royal Highness, Prince George!"* at the top of his lungs, and the company hastily regrouped in order to welcome the Prince of Wales.

Adam, thrusting his way to the front entrance in the hope of quitting this nauseating event as quickly as possible, most unfortunately jostled against one of Prinny's equerries, putting the man off balance. He in turn fell against the Prince, who might have fallen had he not flung his arms around his hostess, and found himself for a moment supported inadvertently upon her rather massive corsage.

Since massive corsages were universally acknowledged to be Prinny's favorite resting places, the event, from a potential disaster, became the basis of a charming compliment from the Prince, a pleasant surprise for Lady Benedict, and a budgetful of gossip for those guests fortunate enough to have observed the contretemps.

Meanwhile, Adam had managed to fight his way out of the Benedict Town House and summon his own carriage. In the process, he had completely failed to observe a striking female in a dull silver gown of incredible sophistication, who wore a white wig that flattered her huge brown eyes. This attractive female stood staring with dismay at the erratic progress of the peer of the realm who had nearly succeeded in oversetting the Prince.

At Moira's shoulder, Major Norman, resplendent in his full dress uniform, chuckled at the incredible social gaffe.

"You have to admit it," he said with a rueful grin. "Adonis is unique! There isn't another man in London who could knock down the Prince of Wales and make him like it!"

Moira, staring at the incredible scene, had to admit that the Prince, amused and flattered by Lady Benedict's response to his person being flung onto hers, was looking pleased with the situation. Offering his arm to his hostess, he conducted her through the respectful passageway that the guests opened for him into the ballroom. The company then crowded in behind, anxious not to miss a single moment of the royal visit.

Moira turned to her soldier. "May we go home now, Sly? I think I have a headache."

Heartache, more like, surmised the major. And then, grimly, What will it take to make the foolish girl realize that the man's a hollow reed?

"Wait for me in the cloakroom," he instructed her. "I'll tell the Hassletons we are leaving."

Depositing a subdued girl in the custody of the cloakroom maid, Sly made his way through the throng with soldierly dispatch until he found the Hassletons. Henry was delighted at the presence of the Prince, to say nothing of all the other nobs, and stood talking loudly with a group of his own friends.

"This is something like . . ." he was telling Lili when Sly located them. Nodding at the soldier, he included him in the conversation. ". . . I must admit, though, that I'd expected better victuals at a great house like this, Major! *More* and better, considering the amount they choused me out of for the subscription," he grumbled.

Lili giggled shamelessly, and Henry's fellow merchants chuckled agreement. Even the soldier was forced to restrain a grin at the open disappointment on Henry's face.

Lili regarded the military figure with knowing eyes. He really would be a splendid match for Moira. Lili had made a few discreet inquiries, and was aware of the small, neglected estate, the major's lack of funds, and his fine war record. Henry must be wheedled into putting up a substantial dowry for Moira, who might then marry her soldier and settle comfortably into county life—which Lili was convinced was the proper setting for her young, unsophisticated cousin.

With these benevolent thoughts in mind, Lili glanced beyond Sly's shoulder. "Moira is not with you, Major?"

"She has the headache," explained Sly. "I left her in the ladies' cloakroom while I came to ask if I might be permitted to see her safely home."

Henry fussed at this evidence of female weakness at such an inappropriate time. "Missing her chance to see and be seen, is she? You'll never get her fired off this way, Lili," he predicted gloomily. "Well, I shall just have to eat her share of the refreshments—that is, if I can find any at offer," he grumbled.

Lili, eyes sparkling, nodded her permission to the waiting officer, who vanished into the press without further ado.

"You want to keep an eye on that soldier," warned Henry.

"Oh, I have," Lili told him. "He will do very nicely

for my cousin—if I can get her mind off that spoiled hot-headed nobleman long enough to recognize a real man when she sees one!''

Henry had always had a great deal of respect for his wife's know-how, and merely nodded and said he'd be happy to leave all the details to her. After all, the girl deserved something for her plan to renovate the guildhall. He was, however, much more interested in a juicy bit of scandal that had drifted its way around the crowded rooms.

''Did you know that Donat knocked his heir down and broke his nose?'' he whispered.

''That must have been before he knocked the Prince into Lady Benedict's arms,'' grinned Lili. ''You have to give the man credit, Henry. He knows how to liven up the dullest party!''

In the comfortable Hassleton coach, which Sly had requisitioned with true military dispatch, the soldier ventured to place a respectful arm around Miss Lovelace's soft shoulders.

''To keep your head steady,'' he explained gently, his mouth so disturbingly close to Moira's ear that his warm breath touched her cheek.

''My head?'' asked the girl, and then, ''Oh! The headache!'' Ever honest, she began with difficulty, ''I must admit—''

''Never admit anything,'' the old campaigner advised. ''I understand. You are—safe with me.''

With a thrill of surprise, Moira realized that that was nothing less than the truth. She *was* safe with Hilary Norman, safer and better protected than she had ever been in her life. She stared up at his strong, weathered face in the gloom of the carriage. How darkened his skin was by the campaigns he had fought! The first inklings of what he might have had to endure crossed her mind: the cold, comfortless bivouacs, the poor and meager food; above all, the constant cruel risk of life and limb day after day, night after night! The *battles!* What had they been like? Her eyes traced the strong features with unconscious tenderness. The

140

white slash of his predatory grin, with its narrow upper lip and sensuous lower fullness, was missing at the moment. His odd silver gaze was intent upon her own features.

Suddenly the man pulled her closer—so close, in fact, that the hard excrescences of his buttons dug rather painfully into her soft flesh—and said in a gravelly voice, "I want the right to . . . to keep you safe. Always." His fine dark head bent closer to her face.

Yet he waited. Held himself in leash until the girl gave the word that his attentions would not be distasteful to her. Moira marveled at his self-restraint. So different, her mind told her, from Adonis, who never bothered to deny any impulse that struck him, however wayward. The girl frowned.

Catching the shadow of movement across Moira's face, the soldier cursed himself for a presumptuous fool. Had he spoiled everything by overeagerness? He held the girl firmly in his arms, unwilling to give up the territory gained, yet fearful to hazard all on an ill-advised advance.

Surprising herself and shocking the nervous soldier, Moira leaned up and planted a soft kiss against the man's hard, warm lips. Then, before he could recover enough to exploit his advantage, the girl gently but firmly removed herself from his grasp.

"I know how much I owe you, Sly," her soft voice came to him in the gloom. "But this is not the time nor the place to discuss it. When we have the guildhall dinner safely behind us, and the problem of the attack on the marquess solved . . ."

Sly settled back against the velvet squabs with a frustrated grimace. Either she didn't want him and was too kind to say so, or she wanted that damned Adonis and was too shy to say so—or she didn't know *what* she wanted, and would need a strong man to help her make up her mind!

Encouraged by this latter idea, Major Norman undertook to entertain his companion with lighthearted conversation for the rest of the trip to Queen's Square. After seeing Miss Lovelace safely within the mansion, Sly returned the carriage to Benedict Town House, to be ready when the Hassletons needed it. Grinning, he strode off, amusing himself with the picture of Henry ransacking the Benedict kitchens for enough food to satisfy his hunger and his sense of a fair bargain.

It was very late indeed when the Hassletons returned home, but Lili came softly into her cousin's room in spite of the hour. As she had expected, Moira was still wide awake. Lili seated herself cozily at the foot of the girl's bed and smiled into the wide, weary brown eyes.

"He loves you," she said quietly.

"But the—*other* does not," returned Moira sadly.

"The marquess is unable to love anyone but himself, at the moment," Lili acknowledged.

Moira sat up straight, her soft brown hair like a flowing cape over her shoulders and across her breasts. " 'At the moment'?" she repeated. "You think he might learn to love . . . someone . . . someday?"

Lili gave a very Gallic shrug. "*Qui le sait?* Who knows? But it will be a very painful process, and I think he will *resent* her who teaches him as much as he will love her. And it is sure that Adonis's idea of *love* will never be the same as yours, my innocent!" The older woman stared at Moira's anxious little face. "Oh, *p'tite!* He is beautiful, that is true, but he is *un bébé!* And you, I think, deserve a *man!*"

She got up and came to the head of the bed. Gently pushing the girl back against the pillows, she said softly, "You have looked after your parents all your life, cared for every waif and stray you encountered along the way. Is that not so? It is time you learned the other half of love, and let a strong man care for you for a change. Good night, child."

Moira lay awake for a long time, thinking about the many faces of love, and a difficult arrogant man who might be taught to love someone other than himself—someday. When she finally fell asleep, she dreamed of kissing Adam Donat, and awoke with tears on her cheeks.

CHAPTER NINETEEN

Two days after the Benedicts' charity ball, the marquess received a summons from Bow Street while he was enjoying a late and leisurely breakfast. The missive did not seem to admit of argument or negotiation. Driving gloomily through the raucous streets and alleys of early-morning London, Adam wondered what fresh insults fate had in store for him. He would have given heavy odds that Vivian, in a vengeful mood, had gone whining to the authorities about the well-deserved punishment Adam had meted out. Well, if that was all—! No man had a right to announce to half of London that his cousin was a murderer! The little weasel deserved his broken nose!

When Adam was finally face-to-face with the magistrate, however, he discovered that the case was far different, and more serious, than he had supposed.

Sir John Benedict had disappeared from his home—had not been seen for at least forty-eight hours. His parents, busy with their charitable entertainment, had not really missed him. After all, he was twenty-five-years-old, more than capable of managing his own affairs—and disdainful of theirs. He did still live at home, however, and had not been seen in his rooms or out of them since the evening before the ball. Neither his portmanteaus nor any of his clothing was missing. His valet finally managed to get the ear of Lady Benedict, who, in turn, aroused her rather ineffectual husband to action. The latter had sent a groom to inquire at the various clubs and known haunts of his worldly son, but for some reason, the Benedicts had not been in touch with their son's best friend.

When Lord Benedict's inquiries proved fruitless, he had reluctantly called at Bow Street to consult the magistrate, Mr. Rowley. Who, upon discovering that the missing man's best friend had not been questioned, at once sent for him.

The marquess was received by a sergeant. In a businesslike manner, the officer invited Lord Donat to take a chair, and almost before the ruffled nobleman had seated himself, the sergeant asked, "Would you have any idea of Sir John Benedict's whereabouts, my lord?"

Startled, the marquess snapped, "Of course I have not! I am not Benedict's nanny! More than likely he's off somewhere with a ladybird. And I promise you he won't thank you for interrupting him at *that* sport!"

The sergeant made no comment but wrote busily in his commonplace-book. Adam began to fume at the delay, the imposition upon his valuable time for something that should have been handled by John's parents; the *insolence* of the fellow, keeping Adam Donat kicking his heels in this grimy little office! He rose to his feet with an oath.

"One moment more, my lord, if you please," said the sergeant quietly.

Adam found himself sitting down again. The look in the fellow's eye, while perfectly respectful, was strangely hard.

"We have received a report that you, my lord, were seen talking to Sir John outside Watier's club the night he went missing. You may, indeed, be the last person who spoke to him before he—disappeared. Would you care to tell us what you gentlemen discussed during that meeting?"

Adam stared at the officer in shocked dismay. He had the oddest feeling that some sort of noose was tightening around his throat. First Nims's murder—ascribed to Donat by an unknown intellingencer. Now John's disappearance. Frantically he tried to remember whether he had, indeed, met and talked with John Benedict three nights ago. Surely not! He had been wary of his best friend after the aspersions that Beresford had cast upon John's actions and motives!

144

Incredibly, Adam found himself stammering under that hard, intent gaze. "Three nights ago? I think not. I do not recall speaking with Benedict since . . . since . . ." He pulled his wits together and glared at the Runner. "I demand to speak to Samuel Beresford," he said.

An hour later Adam faced his old friend across the desk in Beresford's private chambers. The lawyer was frowning.

"There's more to it than they told you, Adam," Beresford advised him. "They've had a letter charging you with murdering Benedict and disposing of his body."

"But that is—insane!" gasped Adam.

Beresford nodded. "I'm inclined to think your enemy has grown tired of trying to ambush you, and is now endeavoring to prod the authorities into doing his dirty work for him."

"But *who*—?"

"It's past time we discovered that fact," said the lawyer grimly. "Our prime suspects seem to be reduced to two: Vivian Donat and Max Hightower."

"Or some spiteful female with a hired bully," muttered Adam.

"Let us deal with the more obvious suspects first," suggested Beresford impatiently. "If we work down the list of ladies loved and left, we may never get to the end of this!"

Both men laughed, and Adam felt the better for it.

"I had better tell you," he admitted, "I may have broken Vivian's nose at the Benedicts' charity ball two nights ago."

The lawyer seemed disproportionately disturbed. "What happened?" he demanded.

Adam told him as briefly as possible.

"A splendid heir," growled Beresford. "Calls you a murderer in front of half of London! Still, it is unfortunate that you knocked him down. It will convince the spiteful that you are a violent man, quite without self-control." His minatory glance rested on the sullen, handsome countenance across the desk from him. "Which, of course, is the truth."

Adam was about to object violently, and then decided not to reinforce the lawyer's poor opinion of him with any more displays of unbridled temper. "What should I do?" he asked, meekly enough for him.

"Go home and try to stay out of trouble," said the lawyer shortly. "Above all, do not pick any quarrels with Hightower. It only wants the news that *he's* been kidnapped and you are definitely *in for it*, my dear Donat! And that I promise you!"

An hour later, pacing restlessly in his library, Adam was struck by a provocative idea. In spite of everyone's rejection of the charge, he still clung to the notion that the little Lovelace chit knew more than she had admitted about the attack on his carriage. Reluctantly he had acknowledged that she actually hadn't been a conspirator. Even so, she probably *knew* more about what had happened than she had let slip. Sly, the mysterious stranger, in whose house she had spent the night! Was *he* the mind behind the ambush?

From this titillating suspicion it was an easy step to a decision to seek out the little commoner and wring the truth from her. She must have learned *something* during that long night in Sly's room, no matter how innocent she had been of the major plan of ambush! It should not be so hard to wheedle the country spinster into betraying all she knew, Adam told himself with a sneer. He'd never failed with a woman yet!

In his eagerness to explore this attractive possibility, Donat ignored the headache that seemed to have become a constant annoyance. Summoning his carriage, he gave John Coachman the spinster's address. He intended to get the Lovelace woman alone, away from the protection of her plebeian relatives, and force a confession out of her. How could this be accomplished? Why, in his own carriage, of course! He'd have the two servants as chaperons in case she tried to run a rig on him, and he would have the secure closed space to pin her down and make her accede to his demands . . . for information, of course!

Sitting back comfortably against the velvet squabs, the

marquess contemplated the situation with more pleasure than he had felt for several weeks.

He was smiling when he entered the door of Queen's Square. Pomfret, concealing his disapproval, deposited Milord in the formal drawing room and then went to announce Moira's visitor to her. The girl hastened downstairs, heart beating rapidly. The marquess was at his most urbanely charming.

"Forgive my intrusion, dear Miss Lovelace, but I thought you might enjoy a breath of fresh air after the rather overpowering crush at the Benedicts' reception. And I dared to hope you might show me that you had forgiven my rude behavior by permitting me to drive you out in my carriage?" He was using his most successful, wheedling tones, half laughing, half humble, and his most dazzling smile.

Forgetting everyone's warnings and her own rationality, Moira agreed with enthusiasm. Perhaps dreams did come true? She returned to her room, donned a pretty brown velvet mantle and a tiny hat with brown velvet ribbons, and within five minutes was being helped into Milord's massive carriage. As she settled herself against the soft upholstery, she sighed with pleasure.

"What an excellent idea! So kind of you!" she murmured.

Adam's grin was feral. "You do forgive me, then?" he murmured, in the voice that had proved irresistible to every woman he had ever set his sights on. An accomplished man-about-town, he did not deem it necessary to devise an elaborate stratagem for the seduction of Miss Moira Lovelace. His unbroken record of successes with the female sex had perhaps made him too self-confident. In any case, he moved directly into the speech and actions that had always brought him everything he ever wanted from her sex. It never occurred to him that the country mouse might be a different breed of cat.

His first move, when the footman had closed the heavy door and the magnificent carriage was rolling along the street, was to take Moira's hand in his and inspect it carefully (an action that always made females feel a little insecure), and then raise it gently to his lips. At this point, Adonis always directed a long, languishing look into the woman's wide, flattered eyes.

Unfortunately, it was hard to see Moira's eyes in the gloom of the coach, and especially under the brim of the hat.

Adonis placed his usual soft kiss on the rosy palm, then replaced her hand in her lap, managing to trail his fingers as though by accident across her skirt as he did so.

Moira blushed.

His smile wider, Adonis carefully placed one large arm across the girl's shoulders. "Rest your head," he advised softly.

Moira chuckled.

Startled by this response, the marquess peered down at her. "You are amused?" He could hardly believe it. It was not the effect he usually had on women.

"Forgive me," begged Moira, smiling, "but that speech and gesture seem to be required behavior for a London gentleman who is driving a lady in a carriage!"

"Behavior?" For the first time in his adult life, Adonis was confused. He strove for normality. "You mean, some other gentleman has been putting his arm around you in his carriage?"

"*And* advising me to rest my head," Moira agreed, grinning naughtily. "I suppose it is one way to get a woman's head on your shoulder." She chuckled again. "Better than getting one over a barrel—*oh!*" Moira, less poised in the situation than she had tried to appear, cut off her silly teasing when she realized what she had just said—and to whom. It was *Sly* with whom she felt enough *at home* to share the joke of the innkeeper's barrel.

Quite a different gleam now sharpened Adonis's languishing violet gaze. So the little witch liked a ribald joke, did she? So much for simpering airs and graces! Down to business! Lunging forward, he seized the rosy-faced girl in his big arms, pulled her roughly against his chest, and took her lips in a crushing kiss. After a long, gratifying moment

148

he began to move his mouth demandingly over her lips. He noted that her eyes were closed, felt her lips trembling and moist against his, grunted his satisfaction. Then he lifted his head, loosened his arms, and moved away slightly from the soft, luscious little body in order to arrange her in a more pleasurable position on his lap.

"So *this* is what you wanted all the time!" he gloated. "You are all alike, you females! Sham innocence! Affected decorum! And underneath—!" His beautiful face was alight with lustful amusement. "So be it, my naughty little angel! Let us pleasure ourselves. I was wiser than I knew, bringing my closed carriage."

Ignoring the wide, shocked eyes in the girl's white face, Adonis began to undo the row of provocative tiny buttons that held the front of the silk dress closed. "Sweetheart, I congratulate you. You really had me bamboozled. When we've had enough of each other, I'll give you cash to set yourself up in a nice little house. There'll be no lack of *custom*, not when Adonis recommends you!"

Moira slapped his grinning face.

"Be good enough to take me home," she said harshly. "I have had quite enough *fresh air*!"

CHAPTER TWENTY

The last few days before the guildhall dinner were the most crowded, demanding, and happy of Moira's life. In a desperate attempt to erase from her mind the humiliating, ugly scene with Lord Donat, Moira had sent a note to Major Norman asking very humbly if she might be of any assistance at all with the work on the guildhall—taking notes, filing accounts, anything. . . .

Sly was a seasoned campaigner. He was easily able to read the desperation between the neatly written lines. As he set out, posthaste, to offer whatever protection or comfort his little love required, he tried to imagine what could have set the darling girl into such a pelter. Could Henry have turned a bit awkward? Sly was sure that Lili was on his side, and probably working to achieve the same end. Setting his lips firmly, the gallant major rode to the rescue.

The trembling warmth and gratitude of Moira's welcome sent a stab of alarm through the major's hard body. *What had happened?* He knew that he must not ask, must not force some unpalatable explanation from his poor little love. His response to her greeting was warm, steady, reassuring—and prosaic. The wily campaigner deemed it better to bring the volatile situation down to basic, unemotional, matter-of-fact—the major caught himself up. He was rambling like a blithering idiot, not acting with manly decisiveness and dispatch! He took a steadying breath.

"I was glad to receive your offer of help," he began, in a voice whose prosaic calm he admired. "Things are rather hectic at the hall—and do not think you can escape the penalties of your generous action in landing me with the job!"

He was pleased to observe that his easy banter was already removing some of the look of pain in the lovely little face lifted to his. Lifted. . . . Sly pulled his fascinated gaze away from that delicate rose that was the girl's soft mouth.

"Are you ready to accompany me this very minute to the guildhall?" he demanded cheerfully, and was rewarded by a faint gleam of the beloved smile.

"Oh, yes, Sly," Moira answered devoutly. "I—I have my cape and reticule ready—in case you wished to take me up on my offer."

While he was helping her into her robe, the warm, brown, fur-lined cape he remembered so well, Moira kept up a hurried flow of small talk, asking questions without waiting for answers. When they came out to the street, the girl's eyes lighted upon Sly's neat curricle, and he saw the first spontaneous smile of the day.

"Oh, an *open* carriage! I am so glad!"

Not having knowledge of the ugly scene in the marquess's closed vehicle, Sly was unable to make much sense of this remark, but he did his best, saying easily, "Oh, my curricle, like my character, is an open—er—book. Shall we leaf?"

Chuckling, Moira groaned dramatically. "Not if you intend making any more such terrible puns, Major!" she said. And then, sobering, she clasped the hand he had offered to boost her into the curricle.

"I am so glad you needed me today, Sly," she confessed softly. "I—I needed *you*—"

Controlling his delight, Sly boosted her up into the seat of the dashing vehicle with only a laughing comment.

"Oh, you may regret this day's work before you've finished the day's work," he said outrageously. "I have *plans* for you, Miss Lovelace! I am glad you wore your *sensible* clothing to this job, for it is becoming the most irrational mishmash of frustrating frustrations I have ever encountered. If the stonemasons are not shouting objections to the mess made on their freshly polished slabs by the nasty paste of the metalworkers (used, I may tell you, to brighten the lead that *they*—the metalworkers—had just poured into the coats of arms that the stonemasons had just incised in the stone slabs) . . . Where *was* I?'' Sly demanded, querulously.

"Polishing the lead,'' supplied Moira with a wide grin. "Or perhaps polishing the stone. I am not quite sure. Your polished discourse overwhelms me!'' and she chuckled lightheartedly.

Sly, tooling his vehicle neatly through the busy streets, heaved a sigh of relief. Whatever had so saddened and shocked his darling, she was able to throw it off for the moment to join him in silly wordplay.

"You have scarcely heard the beginning of our problems,'' he warned her. "Next we have the glaziers, who are screeching that the new panes of glass they were to reset are the wrong size, or the wrong shape, or the wrong thickness—''

"Or the wrong color?'' ventured the girl, smiling.

"You are in league with them,'' accused Sly, darkly.

Moira's head was whirling, but her heart was lighter than it had been for days. *Friendship!* That was the thing to value in life! Not girlish adoration, surely not passion! These were cruel betrayers, humiliating, degrading! Friendship such as that offered so generously by Major Norman was the greatest gift a woman could receive. And she had Sly's friendship! The girl sat back at ease in the high-wheeled, elegant little curricle and prepared to enjoy a day of satisfying, useful endeavor.

The first crisis that faced them as Sly led her into the guildhall was a screeching altercation. It seemed that a minor riot had erupted when the scrubwomen arrived to find that dozens of cartons of new dishes had been brought in and stacked all over the dirty kitchen floor just as they were required to wash it! Moira freely admitted, battered as she was by shouts of anger, yells of encouragement from the stonemasons, and ribald cries from the metalworkers, that she could not have handled the situation.

The major took charge, however, with good humor and authority. He was here, there, everywhere. Unfailingly courteous, yet unshakably firm, he dealt with the scrub-women's problem, got the different guilds back on the job, and shortly had the mutually suspicious teams working in real, if occasionally noisy, harmony.

And so it went, those last crowded days. Moira came into the hall on the final morning to find everyone working with a will to the beat of a marching song. Holding the sheaf of accounts Sly had requested in one hand, and the small piece of colored glass that had been missing from the final section of window in the other, the girl paused a moment to enjoy the rousing chorus. She soon perceived that the words being lustily bellowed out by every male present, including Sly, were more than a little bawdy.

So that is the kind of music men sing to hearten them for battle, she thought, searching Sly's face with a tenderness she was not aware of. At that moment, the lean, hard body, coatless, more than a little dusty, turned, as to a magnet, in her direction.

Sly strode toward the girl, his smile widening into a grin of delight as he caught the fleeting expression of warm admiration in her gaze. His eyes alight with laughter, he said primly, "To what do we owe the pleasure of this visit, ma'am? I must warn you, this is a *men's* club!"

The surrounding artisans were eavesdropping shamelessly, grinning at the fun, well-pleased at what they had accomplished.

Moira entered into the spirit of the final, successful *push.* She waved both hands aloft. "The final pane of glass!" The glaziers cheered. "The drafts to pay the workers!" This time the cheers were deafening, and the men surged forward to surround the two.

"Is that all?" sniffed Sly outrageously. "I thought you had something *important* to tell us!" He seized her arm firmly.

"Oh, I do have a suggestion," Moira retorted. "It is from the Houses of Parliament. They wish you to moderate your voices. You are waking up all the Tories in the House!"

The men accorded this thrust the laughter it deserved. Moira waited for Sly to unhand her, but his hard, warm fingers remained clasped firmly above her elbow. He assumed a grimace of deep distress. "What? No word of praise for our splendid accomplishments? No thanks for all our efforts? You truly disappoint me, ma'am!"

Moira took her time gazing around the busy, crowded hall, and smiling at the pleased male faces ringing the major and herself. When at length she spoke, there was no mockery in her voice. "You all have accomplished wonders! *Well-done!*"

Pleased, yet not wishing to show it, Sly shrugged off her genuine admiration. He took the pane of glass from her gently, and handed it to a waiting glazier. Then he accepted the drafts, and thrust them into his shirt, patting the bulge solemnly.

"This little blessing shall be delivered to you when you have finished work, tonight," he advised the eager workers.

No one seemed ready to go back to work. The men were waiting for something, Moira was sure of it. What could it be?

Apparently the drama between herself and the major had still to be resolved. The major spoke first.

"Although you might scarcely credit it, I promise you the hall will be ready to receive the Honorable Mrs. Barton's guests by tomorrow night."

Moira took a long look around the scene of dust and confusion, shook her head, smiling, and tried to move away from the major's firm grasp. He did not release her arm. Puzzled, the girl stared up into the dark, smiling face. He was not angry, that was plain. And he could not have *forgotten* that he was holding her arm, could he?

"Was there something else?" she asked uncertainly.

"My reward," said the soldier clearly. "You have neglected to reward me for my sterling services. It is customary."

154

Torn between amusement and annoyance—for they stood in a circle of grinning workmen—Moira tugged ineffectually at his firm clasp. Betraying color rose in her cheeks, to be observed with satisfaction by her captor.

"My reward," repeated the soldier, grinning too complacently.

He knows I dare not create a fuss in so public a place, thought the girl, viewing the wretch's smug expression. She glanced desperately around, considering her alternatives. And then her bucolic sense of humor, which Moira could not always control, surfaced. In a lightning maneuver that would have delighted that excellent strategist, the Duke of Wellington, she threw both arms around the astonished major, crying out in tones that pierced even the workmen's racket,

"Beloved! I shall not abandon you and your child!" and she pulled away far enough to pat the bulge of papers beneath Sly's shirt.

For one instant the major stiffened under her embrace, while a roar of laughter rose from the circle of workers. Then Sly caught Moira to him with both arms in the most enthusiastic hug she had ever experienced. He bussed her warmly, and then, as he gave her a little freedom to breathe, he whispered, "I'll teach you to play off your tricks on me, you little wretch!" He took possession of her lips again in a kiss whose masterly technique startled her into dazed immobility, able only to accept, to receive, to—wonder at the glory of shared joy!

Moira was brought back to a sense of her surroundings by the sound of loud cheers and laughter. Before she could pull her dazed wits together, Sly released her and set her a pace away from his hard, warm body. They were the focus of every eye in the vast hall, Moira knew.

She stepped forward and pressed a hot, sweet kiss upon Sly's dear, treacherous, exciting mouth. Holding his darkly handsome face between her palms, she surveyed it with stern warning.

"And that is all the reward you are going to get, sir!

155

And very generous—considering your condition!'' and she patted the papers again.

Releasing him, she walked triumphantly out of the hall, to the sound of a cheer led by the irrepressible Sly.

While she was being driven back to the Hassletons' in a hired hackney, Moira found herself comparing kisses. A few days earlier, she had been rudely bussed inside the closed carriage of the Marquess of Donat. Admittedly she was no connoisseur, and she had to confess that she had dreamed of Adonis kissing her, holding her in a close embrace. Yet when it had happened, it had been not only humiliating, given his assumptions as to her purpose and lack of virtue, it had also been strangely . . . *unsatisfying*! More like a puppy's hasty, graceless licking than a grown man's loving caress—or so she now thought. Her big brown eyes opened wider as she realized that she was comparing Adonis's wet slobbering with the hard, sweet pressure of those lips she had just encountered. It had been, she realized, a pleasant, even an exciting, experience. She actually wanted more! To explore that controlled, masculine ardor, which was so reassuringly tender and supportive—and yet not weak or *namby-pamby*! Oh, not Major Hilary Norman! Moira decided, rather happily, that she would call her friend Sly by his real name—Hilary—from now on. He really deserved a better cognomen than Sly!

Her euphoria lasted until she went in to dinner that night with the firm intention of reporting on Hilary's brilliant handling of the guildhall restoration. Henry blossomed under the good news, and made some pretty revealing comments about his own ambitions, now more likely of accomplishment than ever before.

"I owe most of it to you, Moira, I'm willing to admit," he said kindly. "If you hadn't run into that crazy nobleman and hired Major Norman to deliver him safe home, we'd never have met Sly!" In the sudden silence that followed his remark, the girl caught a warning glance passing from Lili to her too-voluble husband. Henry at once turned the conversation back to the details of the refurbishing process.

156

Moira was sure Adonis had been behaving badly again and might have tried to quiz Lili as to the details had she not been really more interested in the wonderful work Hilary was doing than in the careless or arrogant behavior of the man whose lustful embraces had shocked and offended her.

There were so many last-minute, urgent details concerning the following night's dinner to be discussed, correct procedures to be reviewed, and threatening disasters to be averted, that nothing except the guildhall celebration was even mentioned during the meal. And afterward, leaving Henry to his port, Lili took Moira to her boudoir for an important discussion. She announced that she was having second thoughts about the delicately romantic gown Moira had planned to wear to the dinner. Camille's brilliant improvisation, the silver-net overdress, had achieved such a surprisingly modish effect at the Benedict charity ball, that it seemed to Lili to be the stronger contender. As soon as they were established in comfort in Lili's elegant boudoir, and Pomfret himself had brought up their after-dinner coffee, Lili began to give her arguments.

"The romantic gown"—for so they had both taken to naming it—"would be perfect for a debut, or a presentation at court, or even . . . a wedding." Catching the expression on her cousin's face, Lili hurried on. "Now, the silver-on-white is *different*. It might even set a style. And it is really more suitable for the guildhall than that—"

"Wedding dress," repeated Moira glumly. "I see your point. Most unsuitable for a spinster-orphan. But I have worn the silver already, and you said—"

"You were in the Benedict house only a few minutes! You had hardly entered the drawing rooms! Who saw you in that crush?" Lili demanded. "I can't even remember what I wore myself that night! If anything!"

Amid laughter, it was agreed that Moira should present herself in the silver-on-white, with the addition of the rosy sash, but without the wig.

"That was most effective for the ball, but this is a VERY SOLEMN OCCASION, *ma p'tite!*"

Moira, remembering the major's scandalous behavior

that afternoon, was understood to say that she hoped some-one had warned *Hilary*!!

As if on cue, Pomfret came in to announce Major Norman waiting below to see Miss Lovelace. Lili, highly pleased, shepherded the girl downstairs, pausing only long enough to make sure she looked her best before she let her go. After briefly but cordially greeting their guest, Lili made her excuses, to the obvious relief and gratitude of the soldier. Moira, smothering a grin at the memory of her own shrewd riposte to his raffish behavior, wondered if something had gone wrong at the guildhall after her departure.

Major Norman soon disabused her mind of that notion.

The soldier had seen the light after his adorable little temporary employer had left him in the middle of a grinning ring of workmen that afternoon. It had struck him that the best—the *only* foolproof way to protect and serve the darling girl was *to marry her* at once, without delay!

Dazed at the stunning, unassailable *rightness* of this revelation, Hilary Norman had stood with his mouth ajar until jocularly challenged by one of the departing scrubwomen.

"Why'n'cha ask her to marry ye, then?" teased the woman. "Keep yer child in the family, like!" and the old woman went off into gales of laughter.

Relaxing with a sense of the absolute correctness of this advice, Sly beamed at his adviser and strode purposefully out of the great hall. Of course, he must go first to his own house and wash off the dust and grime of the day. Then, dressed in his best clothes, he must eat a nourishing meal to give him—strength—courage—whatever it took to chance his luck.

He tried and failed to eat a meal in his empty kitchen, seeing only a vivid little face with sparkling big brown eyes wherever he looked. The witch had put a charm on the place! And then, almost too soon, he was entering the Hassleton mansion and asking the fatherly butler to announce him. While he was still trying to plan out a strategic attack, she was here, his adorable little charmer. And it was going to be all right! For how could anything so man-

158

ifestly *destined by fate to be,* not occur? The major, riding joyously on the wave of his dazzling vision, advanced on his objective with more force than finesse.

Moira, coming happily to welcome her executive officer, found herself seized in an iron-hard embrace. "When shall we be married, my little love?" demanded her captor in a curiously strangled voice.

First startled, and then reminded of the way they had parted, Moira decided her teasing friend was carrying on the jest. Of course, this was his way of paying her back for the outrageous trick she had played on him in front of the raucous audience this afternoon.

"Next Tuesday?" She prolonged the game. "I think I could fit you in."

The major frowned. Why was she making a joke out of his proposal? Surely a girl should behave in a more solemn way at so important a moment? Still, it was the first proposal he had ever made. He released the fragrant, soft body and stepped back a pace. "You take a man's most important offer rather lightly, Miss Lovelace," he said sternly. "I had not expected—levity."

Moira gasped. "You . . . you *meant* it?"

Major Hilary Norman bowed. Rather distantly.

Moira's thoughts were in a turmoil. Hilary wished to *marry* her? Could it be possible? This was her first proposal. She wondered frantically what she should do. It was plain from his withdrawal into cool displeasure that she had deeply offended him. And yet . . . *marriage*! The girl scrambled for something to say.

"I have no dowry" was what came out, shocking her own ears almost as much as it did his.

"I was not aware that such a subject had been mentioned," the officer said, even more stiffly. "I believe I should be able to support you. Perhaps not on the scale to which you are becoming accustomed. . . ." His glance, almost accusing, took in the overostentatious furnishings of Henry Hassleton's drawing room.

Moira felt a stir of anger. "You know very well I am not accustomed to anything more than a small cottage in a tiny village!'' she said hotly—but the heat was for his dismaying change of attitude, not for his words spoken, that she knew, were a hurt response to what *he* had thought *she* meant when she had implied—oh, it was too absurd! This was not her friend Sly! This stiff, angry man was not even darling Hilary, about whom she was already feeling some very unusual emotions. Anxiously she scanned the dear, handsome face she had kissed so pleasurably just a few hours earlier. Could she bring back *that* man . . . ?

Impulsively Moira stepped forward, pulled his stern dark face down to hers, and kissed him soundly. In order to gauge his reaction to her boldness, she kept her eyes wide open.

Sly was doing the same. First the blood seemed to flow out of his head, leaving him dizzy and shaken. And then, with a rush, it flowed back, and he caught his frightening little temptress close in his arms.

''What the *devil* are you playing at?'' he panted against her lips. A most enigmatic smile was on her sweet, soft rosy mouth. He shook her slightly, not so much that he lost his grip, but enough to remind her who was the aggressor in this mysterious game. And then his muscles relaxed. *Aggressor?* He would be lucky if he got out of this with his brains intact! His little charmer had a decidedly alarming effect upon a man who thought of himself as a trained and battle-honed strategist.

''I surrender!'' gasped the major, and put his mouth back where it longed to be, against those rosy lips.

Which, thank heaven, softened and opened to receive his adoration.

After a long moment of extreme delight, Hilary Norman was able to murmur, ''I take it that means yes?''

''Yes,'' said Moira very quickly, so that he would not entangle them both in some other masculine foible or ritual. ''Yes, I will marry you, Hilary. But perhaps,'' she added cautiously, ''we had better wait until after the guildhall dinner to tell Henry and Lili.''

The major, holding his future in his arms, was too blissful to question the delay.

CHAPTER TWENTY-ONE

Moira, busy in the kitchen, was denied the sight of the great carriages swaying and swinging to a halt in front of the guildhall the following evening, when the important figures in the city of London rallied to support Mrs. Barton's restoration ball, as it had come to be called. Between real gratitude that they had not had to squelch out into sodden fields (it had been pouring rain since noon), and pleasure at the sparkling fresh appearance of their historic jewel of a hall, the guests were generous in their praise as they greeted their hostess, and the lord mayor, and the committee headed by Mr. and Mrs. Henry Hassleton.

Moira had arrived two hours earlier, to be sure the food for the lavish banquet was ready, savory, and sufficient. She had hurried past the fourteen-foot-high carved wooden figures of Gog and Magog that flanked the door leading to the Council Chamber, casting those two defenders a wary glance as she did so. Carved in 1708 by one Richard Saunders, to replace an earlier pair made of wicker and pasteboard, the hollow giants were formidable guardians, and seemed, with their lowering frowns, to be challenging Moira's right to be making free use of the guildhall. She almost found herself explaining that she was working in their behalf, to preserve and beautify the historic building. Shaking her head at her own gullibility, the girl walked quickly on to the kitchens to make sure all was perfection for the banquet.

161

When the guests began to pour in, Lili came to find Moira, greeting her with flashing delight in her black eyes.

"Henry is so puffed up with pride that I fear he will swell until he is as huge as those wooden giants—hideous things, are they not? Why one would wish to flaunt *them*!—and will probably burst!" she whispered. "Several of the aldermen have congratulated him on his *brilliant idea* of refurbishing the hall. And Mrs. Barton is telling everyone how hard *she* has had to work to make Mr. Hassleton's idea a reality!" Lili smothered a laugh. "Do you mind sharing the glory? You and the major will have to congratulate each other, since no one else is likely to know who is truly responsible for the triumph."

Moira forced a smile. "If only the dinner goes well . . . and nothing outrageous happens!" She crossed her fingers superstitiously.

Lili was looking past the girl's shoulder. "I do believe I see the marquess of Donat! What on earth can *he* be doing at a plebeian affair like this?"

Moira turned quickly. Adam Donat stood just within the hall, scowling and searching the huge, crowded room with an angry glare.

Oh, heavens, he is in one of his rages! Moira thought despairingly. What can it be this time? Will he try to punish me publicly for slapping his face?

Her jaw set. I shall not let him ruin this triumph for Henry and dear Lili! Impulsively she began to thread her way among the chattering groups toward the marquess.

Major Norman stepped into her path so suddenly that she almost hit his body with her own. Glancing up nervously, she met a hard, questioning stare.

"I advise you to keep away from Donat till the latest charges against him are cleared." His voice was low and hard. "You can see he is angry and dangerous. When he's in one of his furies, he loses control—"

"What charges?" asked Moira, her voice as low as his.

"He is being investigated in the matter of the disappearance of Sir John Benedict, and tonight his heir, Vivian, has also disappeared. The number of suspects is decreasing

162

daily,'' the major ended ironically. There was no use mentioning the letter accusing the marquess of murdering both men. That very afternoon one of Sly's fellow agents, an old army comrade, had been sent to warn the major that he was not to become embroiled in the scandal that was about to rock London.

"Pitt says you've done your best for Miss Lovelace, and must avoid further active participation in so potentially awkward a situation. If one of the P.M.'s agents is known to be meddling in criminal matters—!''

The major set his jaw. "The girl has nothing to do with the damned marquess!'' he had protested.

Only to receive a mocking, "And a great deal to do with you, old man? Better see that *she* stays out of the brouhaha as well! She's no match for Adonis!'' his fellow officer had said. With a sinking heart, Sly stared into Moira's face now, knowing that, match or not, engagement or not, his little lioness was at her most protective. Her small, sober countenance was set in fierce determination. Sly did not know that her determination was to prevent the lecherous nobleman from venting his spite upon poor Henry—or even upon Lili and Sly!

The major tried once more. "I warn you, Moira! Reason and logic play no part in Donat's thinking when he is angry. Can you not let the man handle his problems himself? He is titled, wealthy, and old enough to manage his own affairs. He has friends in high places. What help can *you* give such a man?''

If you only knew, thought Moira, it is Lili and Henry and you, my darling, I am trying to protect! She understood that it was jealousy that set that deep frown to grooving his dark soldier's face, jealousy of a man he deemed handsomer and more attractive in every way than himself. She dared not tell her soldier about the ugly incident in the closed carriage, lest it send him into a disastrous conflict with the powerful creature he had just described. Recalling the marquess's icy, silent fury as his carriage made its way back to Queen's Square, Moira knew it was more than likely that Adonis had decided to exact vengeance for her rejection and especially for that slap on the petulant, beautiful face. I cannot let his venom poison my loved ones! I must get him out of here!

While the major, jealous and angry, and Moira, desperate but determined, faced each other in a silent conflict of wills, the marquess caught sight of them. He strode forward and, ignoring Sly completely, seized Moira's shoulder in a grip so painful that she bit her lip to keep from crying out.

"What do you know of this latest accusation, Madam Tease? I suspect that this namby-pamby *concern* of yours is nothing but a mask for your underhanded little schemes!"

His voice was so harsh and loud that heads began to turn to discover the source of the argument.

Sly removed the offending hand with a grip that nearly crushed the marquess's fingers.

"I think it would be better for all concerned if we continued this discussion in a more private place," the major said firmly, but without heat.

Adam glared at the interloper but, after a glance at the avid faces around them, allowed himself to be led into a small anteroom. Before he could launch into another attack, Moira spoke. Trying for a light touch in the hope that it might relieve the tension they were all under, she smiled up into the beautiful, angry face so close above her.

"We should not wish to make a rumpus in front of all those city dignitaries, should we, milord?" she began, mawkishly sweet.

It was the wrong tone to adopt, she saw immediately. Both men stared at her as though she were out of her mind. Then Adam said, "I demand to know whether you and your lover have been plotting to ruin me!"

"You are mad," said the major grimly. "If your situation were any less desperate, I should challenge you to a duel for your filthy accusations. But since this gentle lady seems to care what happens to you, I shall wait until you are cleared of criminal charges before I do so."

"Noble sentiments from a rascal masquerading as an

officer and a gentleman,'' sneered the marquess unforgivably. ''In what pawnshop did you find that gaudy coat?''

Moira caught her breath as she saw the black rage in her soldier's face. ''No, Sly! Don't hit him! You know it will solve nothing!''

''You would defend this—this miserable excuse for an Englishman?'' He looked at the grinning Adonis. ''I won the right to wear this coat when I served under Wellington, sir. While you, milord, were drinking yourself under the table, gaming away your money, and seducing the shopworn mistresses of your best friends.''

''Bravo!'' Adonis clapped his hands as if applauding a fine performance on stage. As he laughed, Moira caught the strong reek of brandy on his breath.

''He's drunk, Hilary! You can't hold this nonsense against him!''

Major Norman had had his fill of both of them: the silly girl who didn't know a real man from a spoiled boy, and the drunken clown she persisted in defending. Blind with jealousy, he drew himself up and favored them with his smartest salute. ''I see I am superfluous in this encounter,'' he said coldly. ''I bid you good night.'' He strode away with a firm tread.

Adonis laughed. ''I have routed your fine hero without having to strike a blow,'' he leered, his violet eyes sparkling with drunken mischief. ''He is only a pasteboard soldier after all!''

Moira held his mocking gaze with steady eyes. After a moment, the grin faded from the beautiful face and Adonis frowned. Drunk as he was, he could sense that the girl was condemning him. How dare she set herself up to judge him?

''You are perhaps the most beautiful human being I have ever seen,'' she said quietly. ''Is there a mind behind that flawless face, a person who makes judgments, true or false, about other people, and acts upon those judgments? Or is there just a spoiled, willful child? If your decisions are proved incorrect, do you try to make amends as decent men do? Inside that magnificent body, where human souls have

165

values, ideals, compassion, are you as empty as the hollow statues of Gog and Magog?'' She turned away.

Donat took a single step after her—whether to kiss or kill he did not know—and felt a sharp rap on one shoulder. Swinging about, Adam found himself eye-to-eye with Major Norman.

"Come back to talk it all over?" gibed Adonis.

"I've come back to finish our business," said the soldier. "Outside, where we won't be interrupted by soft-headed females." Of course, he hadn't been able to leave the little idiot to her fate. But if there must be a scandal, it had better not be allowed to ruin Henry's great hour.

Adam followed the major from the guildhall. Outside, it was still raining. Wretched coachmen who hadn't had the sense to return to their stables were huddled on their boxes under sheltering capes. Sly glanced around with a grimace.

"This is no place to carry on a sensible discussion!"

"Much less a common brawl," gibed Adam. "You might get your pretty coat wet."

"You are a fool—and not half as drunk as you would have me think," retorted the major calmly.

Adam shrugged. In truth, he was losing the brandy-induced lightheartedness, or its boon companion, the warming gust of rage he had been fanning all evening, ever since he had been warned of the new charges against him by one of Beresford's most trusted employees. The lawyer had gruffly advised him to get out of London until matters could be investigated and his name cleared. Beresford had no reliance upon his noble client's ability to handle such degrading and dangerous charges as he was liable to face if he remained in the city.

As usual, Adam had done as he pleased. And now he had a fugitive thought that he might better have followed Beresford's directive! He squared his shoulders and sought to stir up some supportive anger.

"So, toy soldier, what shall we discuss?"

"I hear that your *best friend* is missing," began Sly, "and also your heir. You believe in making a clean sweep, do you not?"

166

Both men were huddled as uncomfortably as the coachmen but lacking the heavy capes the latter sheltered under. Adam flexed his shoulders. "Can't we get inside somewhere? A tavern?"

Sly, who wasn't enjoying the exposure any more than Adam was, managed a pitying smile. "Oh, does a little rain upset you? How fortunate that you were not with us in Spain, or France, or Portugal, where the weather was frequently inclement!"

Gritting his teeth, Adam led the way to a comfortable-looking carriage and yanked the door open. Sly followed gladly, merely waving a soothing hand at the hostile coachman.

"Your employer will never know anything about it," he advised, "and I'll give you something for a drink when we leave."

"From what you just told the coachman, you don't intend to fight a duel in here," sneered Adam.

"We must talk." The major wasted no time. "I do not think you are guilty of any of the crimes attributed to you, Donat, but I do think you are your own worst enemy. You do not do anything but harm to your case with these brawls and public tantrums."

This last word was the push needed to fuel a fine rage in the nobleman. "If you can keep your sickly little busybody out of my way, prevent her from drumming up any more schemes to 'save me,' I shall manage nicely," he said provocatively.

The major surprised him. Instead of the brangle Adam had hoped to start, he got a cold look and the quiet instruction, "*You* had better engage to keep away from Miss Lovelace. It was not she who came searching for you tonight—as we both know."

The two men stared at each other through the gloom of the carriage. Then Sly shrugged dismissively. "This is useless. Good night, milord." Swinging open the door, he paused only long enough to toss a coin to the waiting coachman before striding off down the street.

Adam surprised him.

Leaping down with grace, he ran lightly after his antagonist, calling out *"Norman!"* in a husky voice.

The soldier turned, instantly alert.

There was no mistaking the belligerence in the marquess's stance. The major's gaze went past him to the open doors of the great guildhall. Moira stood there, framed in light, wearing her cape. She was peering anxiously into the flambeau-lighted darkness of the street.

She has come to save him again, thought Sly, and the pain of it froze him for a moment. And then his chance to defend himself was gone. Adam's clenched fist struck just below Sly's ear. The soldier went down onto the slimy cobblestones.

Moira ran forward.

Adam saw her and grinned widely. "He didn't even raise a hand to defend himself!" he gloated. "Your *hero*!"

"He was protecting me," the girl said tonelessly, kneeling to raise the inert figure from the ground into her lap. "Get me a carriage."

"We seem to have played this scene before," taunted the marquess. "With a different villain."

Moira did not even bother to look at him.

After a moment Adam strolled off to requisition a coach for the injured man.

CHAPTER TWENTY-TWO

Sometime later Sly opened his eyes and found himself lying on a comfortable bed, staring up into the pale countenance of Miss Moira Lovelace. He was not, at the moment, best pleased with this lady, and the look he gave her was unfriendly.

"Why are you not in the arms of your hero? Congratulating him upon his . . . strength and valor?"

"Stop that," the little female said calmly. "We both know it's not true. You *spared him* because you thought I was worried about him."

"And were you not?" sneered her soldier. "You cared enough about the belligerent fool to leave the banquet and all your obligations and come out to make sure he didn't get his pretty features damaged!"

"That was not why I followed you," Moira said, gently.

The man was not placated. "Why, then?" he demanded.

Moira deftly applied a cold wet cloth to his swollen jaw. "I hoped to prevent a confrontation," she told him. "He—he might have hurt you."

The major found this less than flattering. "Don't try to gammon me, little one! You've thought of no one but that—male beauty since you first laid eyes on him. *Adonis*, remember? I was there."

"You must think as you wish," answered Moira wearily. "Males make a habit of twisting facts to suit their own prejudices, I have learned. To my mind, the most important thing at this moment is to get you on your feet and safely back to your own home. If you will give me the address, I shall have you taken there as soon as you feel able for the trip."

"Very neat!" sneered the soldier, determined to have his pound of flesh from this maddeningly enigmatic little woman. Just twenty-four hours ago, she had accepted his proposal of marriage with every indication of delight. What was she up to now? Had she had second thoughts on seeing the damned Adonis again? Suddenly he thought he knew what was going on. "You are taking all this trouble so as to protect your Adonis from blame or censure for a cowardly blow behind a man's back!"

"You saw it coming," Moira said tonelessly.

The major set his teeth. At this moment the whole imbroglio seemed an exercise in futility. He pulled himself upright. "I am able to leave now."

He glanced around him and discovered that he had been brought up to the girl's bedroom. At least it could be her bedroom. The colors were soft and feminine, the furniture delicate, the woman-scent unmistakably hers. Why had she brought him here?

He glanced down at his clothing, and from there to the delicate bedspread. "I have got mud on your bed," he announced. "Why did you bring me here?"

Moira ignored that rather pertinent question. "Pomfret, Cousin Lili's butler, felt it wiser to have you here, where only he, the footman who helped carry you, and myself would know of your presence," she explained. "In case the Hassletons decided to come home early."

A reluctant grin forced itself onto Sly's stiff lips. "Can you really see Henry abandoning the scene of his triumph while one alderman remains to congratulate him?" he demanded.

Sharing that smile was one of the loveliest things Moira had ever done. Had he forgiven her, then? Or was this just a truce? Either way, it was better than the cold dismissal that had been inherent in his earlier remarks. Moira gathered up her courage.

"May I come with you, to see you comfortably disposed in your own home?" she asked humbly.

But her former champion was too hurt, too wary, to unbend that far. Getting carefully to his feet, he straightened his muddied coat. "Thank you, that will not be necessary, ma'am. You have compromised yourself sufficiently for one night. It is perhaps just as well you did not make public your engagement to a 'rascal masquerading as a gentleman,'" he quoted bitterly. "I shall bid you good night—and good-bye." He strode from her room a little unsteadily, but every inch the soldier.

It was the following afternoon before Moira learned the full extent of the trouble in which the marquess now found himself. She learned it from a very solemn Mr. Beresford, who had called at Queen's Square with the express purpose of questioning Miss Lovelace as a possible witness to the previous night's events. A pale-faced girl confronted the lawyer in Lili's formal drawing room. The lawyer wasted no time.

"I understand that you had conversation with the marquess at the guildhall last evening, just before the dinner?" he began. "I know of your efforts to assist him . . . and of the less than gracious response my client has made," he added gently.

"I did not help him for a reward," Moira said stiffly.

Beresford nodded. "In spite of his stupidity, his bad temper, and his appalling ingratitude, could you find it in your compassionate nature to help the fellow once more?"

"Of course I shall do whatever I can," Moira answered.

The lawyer seemed satisfied with that lukewarm reply. He went on slowly, "What I am about to tell you . . . what I *must* tell you if you are to understand my problem, is to be held by you in strictest confidence. Only Major Norman, if you can enlist his help after last night's debacle, may share the information I am now going to give you."

Did this slender, silver-haired man know *everything* that went on in London? How *much* did he know about "last

171

night's debacle"? She stared at him with rising alarm. "Perhaps you had better not count upon my—enlisting—the major's help," she warned him. "He is out of charity with me. With good cause," she ended sadly.

'Well, we shall have to see," Beresford said. "The charges now being made against my client, Lord Adam Donat, are: that he murdered his best friend, Sir John Benedict (now missing from his home for several days); that he murdered his intelligencer, Alfred Nims; that he kidnapped and possibly murdered his heir, Vivian Donat; and that he was instrumental in kidnapping his gaming companion, Max Hightower, also missing for several days." Ignoring the girl's gasp of horror, Beresford continued, "Vivian disappeared last night. I was in hopes that you might be able to testify to Lord Donat's presence in your company, and Major Norman's, during part of the evening at least?"

It was a question—and a plea. Moira nodded agreement without a second thought. She had been completely disillusioned concerning the beautiful nobleman, but her heart still held concern for a male who had never grown into full, responsible manhood despite his years. She answered quickly.

"Yes, the marquess sought me out at the guildhall dinner last night. We talked for several minutes. Major Norman joined us, and then both men left together. I joined them later in the street. There was—as I am sure you have been told—an argument."

"I hear that Donat knocked the major down," said the lawyer concisely. "And that you rescued the soldier and bore him off in a carriage Donat secured for you."

"You have been correctly informed," said Moira coldly.

Beresford sighed. "I was afraid of that! Not enough time elapsed, you see," he explained to her worried glance. "If he had been going to kidnap Vivian and carry him off, he had plenty of time to do it after he hit Norman. Vivian is well-known for the fact that he spends most nights at gaming hells in very poor neighborhoods. The better houses, White's and Brooks's, refuse to admit him, even if he is

Adam's heir. It seems Vivian was abducted as he was making his way home from one such den.''

''And the major and I cannot help the marquess to prove where he was,'' mused the girl.

Beresford caught the speculative gleam in her wide brown eyes. Almost smiling, he protested, ''Oh, no, ma'am! You must *not* pretend you were with him last night! It would never do! For one thing, your reputation would be smirched beyond repair, and for another, you would have to swear to it in a court of law, and I cannot quite see you perjuring yourself to that degree! But I thank you for the generous thought.''

''Perhaps Sly—Major Norman—might have seen him later last night?'' suggested Moira. But that was a faint hope, and the lawyer destroyed it.

''Considering the way they parted, ma'am, and the number of coachmen and grooms who witnessed their quarrel, it might be better *not* to tie Major Norman into Donat's late-night activities. Because, you see, Adam has disappeared, too. I had advised him to play least-in-sight, but he never accepts my advice. It is claimed he ran off after murdering Vivian last night.''

Moira could only stare at the lawyer in horror. ''Surely no one believes that!'' she gasped.

Beresford shrugged, his face set in an expression of doubt. ''I would have sworn that Adam was not a murderer,'' he murmured. ''Quick-tempered—*violent-tempered*—yes. But not to the extent of killing another human being. Now your major, for instance, has *proved* his mettle in the field. . . .'' he paused suggestively.

Moira said coldly, ''If I thought you were serious, I should do you an injury.''

Beresford chuckled reprehensibly. ''Just proving a hypothesis,'' he explained outrageously. ''No, Miss Lovelace, I do not think either of your cavaliers is capable of the kind of cold-blooded, wily skulduggery we have to contend with here. But Adam Donat is such a looby that he'll get himself hanged for sure if we don't step in and find the real villain. Are you willing to help me?''

"Of course," said the girl. "But you'll have trouble enlisting Major Norman if you have me on your staff. The major," she said reflectively, "is both angry and disillusioned with me at the moment."

"Could we say *jealous*?" probed the lawyer, which was met with a very repressive look from the lady. He took the hint and got back to business at once.

"Can you tell me anything about the crimes, anything that sticks in your mind as out-of-place, perhaps?" he asked.

The girl pondered the matter. At length she asked, "Was the handwriting checked on the note found in Nims's pocket, the one that was addressed to Adam?"

Beresford flipped open a small notebook. "There have been two notes, actually. One, purporting to come from Nims, which incriminated Adam; the second, received this morning at Bow Street, claiming Adam murdered Nims, Benedict, Hightower, and Vivian, and has now fled the country. Yes, the officers got a sample of Adam's writing."

"And?" the girl urged.

"Both letters were printed. Anyone could have written them."

Moira thought about that. "Surely no one would bother to incriminate Adam unless he—or she—had a vital interest in the Donat estate and title?"

"Like Vivian? But he's disappeared, too."

Moira frowned. "I cannot believe that Adam would be stupid enough to leave a note incriminating himself on the body of a man he had just murdered. The note was *meant* to incriminate him."

"I am inclined to agree with you, Miss Lovelace," said the lawyer. "Thank you for your patience and your help. If anything else occurs to you, will you let me know at my office or my residence, as quickly as possible?" He handed her a slip of paper upon which the two addresses were neatly written, thanked her again, and took his leave.

Moira stood in the drawing room for a time after Beresford left, thinking uneasily that there was something about

174

the matter, something quite simple, which she had failed to perceive. One thing she did know, Beresford had given her a chance to see Sly again!

Fortunately for Moira, the major was at home when she arrived at his house an hour later. She had taken the time to present her best appearance, for she had a pretty good idea that her soldier would not surrender without a brisk battle. It seemed she was right. When the major opened the door, his expression, at first merely curious, became quite forbidding when he recognized his visitor.

"What do *you* want?" he snapped.

Moira considered the possibility of telling him the truth, but decided it was too risky just yet. "To speak to you for five minutes," she murmured instead, venturing a smile.

Sly glared at her suspiciously, and his expression hardened. "Beresford's been to see you, and the two of you have mounted a campaign to rescue your pretty marquess," he accused. "Well, I wish you good luck, but you may count me out," and he made to close the door.

"Hi-i-i-lary," cooed Moira in saccharine tones. *"Please?"*

Almost against his will the soldier grinned.

"Minx," he said appreciatively. Then he stiffened his will. "You aren't going to get around me with any of that wheedling! Find someone else to pull your beautiful idiot out of his self-made mess. I've resigned."

"I need you," said Moira honestly.

Sly glanced at her sharply. There was something in her voice. . . . Then he hardened his heart. A man would be a fool to break his back to secure another man for the woman he himself loved! "Go away, Moira. Let the authorities help him. If he is innocent, he won't suffer."

The lovely girl stared up at him in silence.

Almost unmanned, Sly began to close the door.

"I'll still be here, you know," she said softly. "Standing out here in all weathers, waiting for a crumb from your table . . ."

Sly glared at her. "What are you trying to do to me?" he almost shouted.

175

"I am trying to tell you I want you," the witch said softly.

It did not occur to the beleaguered man that she really meant she wanted *him*. He knew too well that she was besotted over her beautiful marquess. So of course what she wanted was the soldier's *help*. Staring down at that sweet face, Sly gave up the unequal struggle. Shrugging, he stepped back and held the door open. "Come in," he said grimly. "I suppose I shall have to help you, but I must warn you that I have decided to resume work with the government tomorrow. Any help I give must be done today."

"Not long enough," said the little shrew boldly. "You'll have to ask Mr. Pitt for an extended leave of absence."

The major glared at her incredulously. "Where did you come by that knowledge?" he demanded. And then, "No, don't tell me. If you've subverted the whole government, I'd rather not hear about it!"

"I guessed," offered Moira humbly.

"As I said, you are a witch." Gloomily Sly led the way into his small dining room. It was cold and dark.

"You aren't asking me upstairs?" the girl prodded.

"No," said Sly uncompromisingly. "State your problem. Briefly."

"I'm hungry," said Moira.

It was true. She had been so excited at the opportunity of seeing her soldier once more that she had not bothered to eat lunch. "May we go down to the kitchen?" Perhaps their presence in that room might bring back pleasant memories to her disgruntled major?

He was staring at her warily. "You're really hungry?"

"Starving!"

Don't overdo it, the girl warned herself. Sly is no fool. She contented herself with a coaxing "Please?"

Convinced he was being maneuvered, yet quite unable to deny the little enchantress, Sly led the way down the narrow stairs to his kitchen. Moira examined the mess with interest. "I see that your chef is still on holiday," she said blandly. "Is there anything prepared for your luncheon?"

"I made myself a cup of tea when I woke up," Sly said stiffly. "I am not hungry. I had rather a bad headache all night."

Moira's eyes went to the blue and purple bruise on his jaw.

"You'll heal quicker if you eat," retorted the girl. "If you will just sit somewhere out of the way, I'll fix a decent meal for both of us."

She slipped out of her short capelet and the enchanting little bonnet that matched it, placed them neatly on a chair, removed her gloves, set them aside with her reticule, and then surveyed the scene. In a minute she had all the dirty dishes in a bowl in the stone sink and was rinsing off the table. Then she walked into the larder and spent a few minutes examining her resources.

When she came back to the kitchen, it was to see the major seated where she had left him, staring at her with a mixture of curiosity and alarm.

"You really mean to prepare food for me?" he asked.

Moira didn't dignify that with a reply. Instead she began beating eggs and chopping cheese for an omelet.

"Your supplies are limited. You need help with your commissariat, major."

The soldier couldn't think of an answer to that.

Fifteen dazzling minutes later, having witnessed the washing of the dirty dishes, the setting of the table with a cloth he had forgotten he owned, Sly was invited to partake of a mouth-watering omelet.

"Eat," commanded the little female crisply.

The soldier almost saluted. Instead, he gathered the remnants of his aplomb and glanced inquiringly at her empty plate. "Where is your food?"

Moira was already beating fresh eggs into the bowl. "You make omelets one at a time," she said complacently. "Then they are delicate and tender. Eat yours while it is hot."

The major, too bemused to argue, and too tempted by the delicate aroma rising to his nostrils, complied. Shortly the girl was seating herself across from him, with a well-laden plate before her.

"How is—*was* it?" noticing his empty plate.

Sly grinned. "Just as good as you knew it would be! Do you intend to eat *all* of yours? If not . . ."

Moira beamed at him. It was working! They were in harmony again, as they had been that first morning before the marquess had intruded into their lives. Rising, she carried her plate around to his side of the table.

The soldier lounged in his place, his lean, hard body at ease in the chair, his dark face turned up to hers, the wide white slash of his smile welcoming her. "I hope this means you are going to sit beside me," he teased, "as well as sharing that enormous omelet!"

Serving him with a portion of her meal, Moira felt that life could hold no greater joy—well, perhaps a *few* greater. The next quarter hour passed in perfect amity, as Moira did not return to her former position and the major enjoyed her cooking with undisguised relish. Finally he pushed back his chair and faced her.

"We'll talk now, little one. Why are you here?"

The girl hesitated, looking into his dark silver eyes with concern. She had already decided that she would always be honest with this man, no matter the cost to herself. But men were, in the phraseology of South Littlefield, *kittle-cattle*, which meant that a woman had to handle them gently. So she said, "There were two reasons why I came. I think the first one will make you angry. . . ." She hesitated.

The wretch, sipping his coffee, had the effrontery to grin at her. The meal seemed to have restored his spirits to a remarkable degree. Or perhaps, Moira thought hopefully, it was not entirely the food?

"So! Your first reason will make me angry," he repeated. "Do you hope the second will placate me?"

Devil! He is enjoying this! the girl realized. Well, why not? I want him to be happy! She gathered her courage. "I hope so," she agreed.

"Say on," he invited, his strong body plainly relaxed

and more attractive than perhaps he realized. Moira could hardly keep her eyes off him.

"Mr. Beresford called upon me today, as you guessed, and told me a great deal about the ugly events that have been happening. Rumors of four murders, and all to be laid at the door of Adam Donat! By whoever set up the crime. . . ." She paused, but the major made no comment. He merely kept his gleaming eyes fixed upon her face and waited for the rest.

"Mr. Beresford and I agreed that Adam, although immature and quick-tempered, was not capable of coldblooded mass murder," Moira continued in a level tone. "We agreed that there must be another person responsible for this wicked plot. Perhaps the one who set up the ambush the night you and I met."

The major showed both interest and pleasure for the first time. "You recall that night in terms of *our meeting*?"

"What happened later, after we had delivered the marquess to his home, is one of my most pleasant memories," she confessed. "I believed I had made a—a good friend." Somehow she dared not say more . . . yet. Then, in order to get this first part over, she went on quickly, "Mr. Beresford hoped that either you or I could give the marquess an alibi. I said that *I* could not, and that you probably should not be approached after what he had so cravenly done to you." There, it was out!

"Wise of you not to pledge me to that fellow's service" was all that her frustrating companion would say.

Moira continued, "I agreed to report any additional facts I might remember, or any new facts that might come my way, and Mr. Beresford left."

Again the girl waited, but apart from an increasingly feral, white-toothed grin, her soldier made no comment.

"You're going to let me make all the running, aren't you?" she asked finally.

Again, just the grin.

Moira accepted her fate. "Very well, then. I proceed to my second reason for coming to you today."

"I am all ears," said the major pleasantly.

Moira stared at him in exasperation. He *was* going to let her say it, open her heart, make herself forever vulnerable to her splendid soldier. He had asked her once. Any further advances must come from her. She pulled in a deep breath. Well, so be it! She opened her lips—

Sly put his arm around her. "You've come to tell me it is I whom you love, haven't you?" he said softly, his silver gaze steady on her face. "*Not* Adonis, for all his beauty."

Moira gasped. "Was I so obvious?"

"Perhaps I am particularly—ah—sensitive where you are concerned," her soldier explained. He rose to his feet, his eyes still locked on hers. *"Tell me!"*

Only by the faintest roughening of that deep voice could Moira understand how deeply moved her soldier was. She felt she could not keep this wonderful man waiting, uncertain, one second longer. She rose and moved eagerly toward him, into his open arms. As they closed about her, hard, warm, protective, Moira shut her eyes with the bliss of the union.

For a long moment the man held her very close to him, both cradling her and challenging her. The girl basked in the feel of him—the warmth and clean male scent of him. She breathed him in with a ragged inhalation of delight. She was hungry for the ardent pressure of his firm, hard lips on hers. After a moment, she opened her eyes. Surely he was going to kiss her?

"That is what I have been waiting for," breathed her soldier. "For you to look at me . . . to let me see your eyes!" He took her lips like a conqueror, in a kiss of total possession. When he raised his head, "We shall announce our engagement tomorrow," he said masterfully, and kissed the tender smile she gave him.

When she had caught her breath, Moira beamed at her soldier with such delighted satisfaction that the man was startled into a laugh. The girl's pretty eyebrows rose in question.

"You exactly resemble a small kitten who has stolen the

180

cream,'' the major explained. ''Pleased, complacent''—he chuckled—''satisfied.''

''Satisfied? Surely you jest,'' returned Moira naughtily.

Incredulous, charmed, Hilary grinned at her. This was no shallow, conventional miss but a real woman, earthy and witty and vulnerable. And *she wanted him*! Her soldier hugged her in an embrace that left her breathless and joyful. Lovingly she scanned the dark masculine face so close above her own. She had not ever observed quite this expression of contentment—of *homecoming*—on his strong features, before.

In truth, Hilary Norman was almost dizzy with happiness. He had never known such utter contentment, yet even as he marveled at his luck, a twinge of fear struck at him that something—or someone!—might take his happiness away. Life held pain, loss. Life was never perfect. He had learned that fact in a hard school!

He knew how compassionate Moira was. She had come to him today to enlist his help in the rescue—again!—of Adam Donat. It was a task he must accomplish in order to win the treasure he sought—Moira's full love, and attention. Compelling his arms to release the soft, warm little female, he forced himself to consider mundane matters.

''We must get back to your *first* reason for coming to me today,'' he began, trying for a light tone. ''What shall we do to save Adonis?''

Why did she continue to press against him, now that he had set her free? Not that I wish her anywhere else but in my arms, God knows, but it is devilish hard to concentrate upon anything else when I can feel her warmth, and catch the sweet woman-scent of her. . . .

Moira seemed to be considering his question. It was more difficult than she had expected to pull away from the seductive gentleness of his embrace. Pay attention! she chided her unruly emotions.

''Did you know anything about John Benedict, or Adam Donat, or Vivian Donat, or Max Hightower, before the trouble began?''

"Only by hearsay," Sly admitted. "I was not one of their exalted company."

"That is their loss," said Moira, with such conviction that Sly felt eight-feet-tall. "What exactly did you hear?" she went on.

"That Hightower was a drunken fool who gamed away his inheritance to Donat; that Adam was overly generous to his friend John, and that all three of them despised Vivian, who naturally hated them."

"A delightful group," commented the girl. "I am glad you are not part of it!" Sly's spirits rose at the hint that Moira was no longer impressed with Adonis.

"I can understand Adam's dislike of Vivian," he admitted. "That is truly a vicious creature, depraved and greedy. The marquess had a right to be disgusted, and wary of him. Vivian was forever circulating nasty rumors about his cousin, at the same time that he was cadging money from Adam's comptroller. As for Benedict, it is widely accepted that Adam is his best friend—and a very good one. The marquess is known to have helped Benedict out of several financial pinches." The soldier paused, then went on, "There is evidence that Benedict might have been behind at least one of the attacks upon Adam's person."

Moira, shocked, said, "But this is dreadful! The ton must be a bear-pit! A man's best friend, recipient of his generosity, to turn against his benefactor!"

Sly, who had lived longer and harder than his little love, said nothing.

Moira was continuing, "It reminds me of the games the boys used to play in South Littlefield. Bamboozling or flim-flamming, they used to call it. It involved tricking some smaller, weaker child. Even as a little girl, I hated it, but the *men*—fathers, older brothers—seemed to think it was great fun, as well as strengthening to the male character." She bent a minatory glance upon her big soldier, as though holding him responsible for the whole male attitude.

Laughing ruefully, Sly held up both hands in surrender. "I confess we are a sad lot, ma'am, but one has to adopt certain *attitudes*, accept certain *rules*, in order to survive in a difficult world.''

Moira absolved him with a sweet smile. ''I am sure *you* have never behaved with cruelty or malice toward anyone weaker than yourself! In fact, I am living testimony to your compassion, your integrity, your—''

Sly, who could have listened to the litany of praise all day, felt constrained by the rules he had mentioned to cut her short. ''You,'' he said tenderly, ''would bring out the best in any man!''

Unwilling to argue against this tribute, Moira was newly strengthened in her determination never to mention the marquess's reprehensible treatment of her. Instead, she returned to the problem they faced. ''Does it seem to you that someone might have set up a series of *hoaxes*—false threats—against the marquess?''

Sly shook his head. ''Dangerous play, I should think, considering that Donat might easily have been killed each time.''

''Then who would benefit, if he had been?''

''Vivian. But he has disappeared.''

''Who else?''

The major shrugged. ''Benedict, I suppose. He has received many loans, and he is in the will. But, Moira, both those men have disappeared!''

''And so has Adam!'' retorted the girl triumphantly. ''If disappearing exonerates them, it should do the same for *him*! Any of the three *could* be guilty. And Adam has nothing to gain from their deaths, while they have a great deal to gain from *his*!''

The major regarded his little love with respect. ''Why didn't I see that? If it's true, we had better find Adam—all of them—at once!''

May God grant they are not already dead was his unspoken prayer.

The major insisted that Moira accompany him to Bow Street, and that Mr. Beresford be sent for immediately. When the whole group was assembled in Magistrate Rowley's chambers, Major Norman set forth Moira's reasoning about the affair. Having expected incredulity or an argument, he was surprised to discover that Beresford at least had reached very similar conclusions, and that the Bow Street officers were actually working on the same premise. Runners were already unobtrusively searching likely places where the missing men might have been hidden. Beresford admitted that some of his private investigators had been following whatever slight clues they could dig up. Heartened but not reassured, Moira sat in the sparely furnished office, considering possibilities.

"If the criminal is Vivian Donat, would he take his victims to his mama's home?"

Beresford shook his head. "His mama may be—strictly between present company—a vicious leech, but she is no fool. Their manor house is the first place anyone would look."

Knowledgeable smiles from the Runners suggested that they had already surveyed that territory.

"Have the Benedicts a home outside London?" was Moira's next question.

"Yes, and there's no one there except the servants."

Dismayed, the girl tried to think of other alternatives.

The major said quietly, "I suppose the marquess's country estates have been discreetly scrutinized?"

Nods all around answered that question.

Moira lifted her head eagerly. "In South Littlefield," she began, and then hesitated as several pairs of masculine eyes flashed to her. Forcing herself to proceed, she said, "I was speaking to Major Norman about the kinds of games that bullies played on weaker boys in my village. One great lout had a nasty habit of taking the favorite toy of some younger boy and hiding it, but never in the bully's own cottage. He would hide it near the child's home. Then, if the stolen object was recovered, it was always considered that the younger child himself had been careless." She waited, realizing too late how absurd and *female* her idea had been.

In fact, the Bow Street officers were smiling gently, and

184

the major was frowning. But Beresford clapped his hands sharply. "*That's it!* Adam's hunting lodge! The very place!"

"Hunting lodge?" echoed Magistrate Rowley. "I'm sure we had a surveillance on every property the marquess owns, but I don't recall—"

Beresford was up on his feet, eager to set out. "I'll tell you as we go! Time is of the essence here!"

Moira was very pale. "Mr. Beresford is correct. We have already lost too much time."

The magistrate held up one hand. "We shall need to coordinate our plans so we do not rush in, startle our villain, and perhaps—*precipitate matters*," he warned them. "Dangerous men with a great deal at stake may strike out viciously when they are cornered. And there is another thing. I thank you for your assistance, but you must understand and forgive me when I tell you I cannot think it wise for civilians to crowd my men at duties for which the officers are specially trained."

"I, sir, am not a civilian, but a soldier who has seen service under Wellington. I am also, as I have informed you, presently working for Mr. Pitt in espionage—which qualifies me to help you search the criminal out," announced the major firmly. "I shall place myself under your command, sir, but I must insist upon coming with you."

Shrugging, the magistrate glanced at Beresford. The lawyer shook his head. "Too vital a matter for a mere elderly civilian to obstruct," he smiled. "Let me share the information I have about Adam's hunting lodge, and then I shall leave quietly, Your Honor!"

This speech relaxed the tension they were all laboring under. He told them that Adam and John, schoolboys home from Eton on holiday, had spent a great deal of time in some ruins near the chief estate of the Donats. The ruins were disregarded, being quite unimportant either historically or artistically, yet they offered excitement to boys of that age. The main feature was a deep cellar or crypt under the best-preserved part of the structure, which had been a small house of worship for an ancient, unorthodox group.

The boys trapped rabbits nearby, and at that time had referred to the ruins as their hunting lodge.

"I agree with Miss Lovelace," the lawyer concluded. "If a body—or bodies—were found there, near Adam's home, one might well be led to believe he was responsible."

Mr. Beresford wished the company success and left.

Moira sent an impassioned glance toward her soldier. Only the merest flicker of dark eyelashes, the faintest gleam in the silver eyes, told her that he would permit her to accompany him. The girl's heart swelled with love. Never, in South Littlefield or in London, had she met with the full, open acceptance of herself as a person that this man so freely gave her.

I love you, her eyes said. I adore you!

The man gave her a smile that echoed that, and more.

After a quiet consultation with the magistrate, the major offered his arm to Moira, and they left with the quiet thanks of Mr. Rowley in their ears.

CHAPTER TWENTY-THREE

Briefing her as to the Runners' plan of attack, and his own permitted part in it, the major smiled down at his love while he drove his small, hooded cabriolet rapidly toward Queen's Square. He handled the powerful horse and the small vehicle with masterly skill, Moira thought. A competent officer!

"You promised me I could come with you," she reminded him.

"Did I?" her soldier teased gently. "Strange, I cannot recall the words! Quote me the exact quote in which I promised that promise, little battlemaid," he teased.

Moira was ready for him. She gave him a luminous smile. "The language was love," she answered softly. "You must take the words from my lips as silently as you gave them," and she pouted those lips at him with delicious provocation.

Groaning softly, the major capitulated, and kissed her with an ardor that quite took his mind off his driving. After a long moment of sweet communion, he put her firmly from him, and assumed a stern demeanor.

"I am a great fool, you know! It seems I cannot say you nay! But if you are to be my army, you must promise to obey, *without question or hesitation,* when I command you. Your life—and mine—might easily depend upon your instant obedience."

Moira had been grinning impishly during the first part

of his speech, but the possibility that Sly's life might depend upon her behavior wiped off that smile.

"Could I really be a danger to you?" she whispered.

"You could get us both killed," Sly said crisply. "But if you do exactly as I tell you," he relented with a grin, "you might even save my bacon. The danger is that you might become alarmed for my safety, burst in on a confrontation, and distract my attention at a crucial moment."

"I understand. And I promise to do *exactly* as you tell me," Moira said humbly, wishing she had not been so eager to share the dangerous adventure with her soldier. If by some folly of mine I put his life in jeopardy—! It did not bear thinking of!

The soldier allowed her to consider the possibilities in silence. When they reached the Hassleton mansion, they were welcomed by Cousin Lili and Pomfret in committee. Although the butler did not question them, Lili did, and Pomfret stayed well within hearing distance while Mrs. Hassleton was brought up to date on the situation. Lili's reaction was predictable.

"Of course you must not accompany the major, *ma p'tite*! He will have his hands full dealing with those *scélérats*, and would only be hampered by having to look after you as well!"

"If you think I am going to sit safely home while he goes into danger—!" the girl gritted.

Miraculously, the major seemed to feel she might be of real help. "This is not your ordinary battle, fought in the open field," he said quietly. "We shall be creeping up upon the criminal in the dark, with stealth. We don't really know how many of them there may be, or who they are. It is a matter for caution and guile—"

Lili's eyebrows were almost to her hairline as she glanced from the major to Moira. "*Caution and guile*—from *her?*"

Sly grinned, but his eyes were steady and warm on the blushing girl. "I may have need of Moira's quick wits and loyalty, before this battle is won," he said slowly. "And she has promised to obey orders. I know it appears reckless beyond permission to you, but could you bear to let your cousin come with me? It means a good deal to us both. Sharing a campaign, as it were." He seemed to be finding the explanation difficult. "A bond," he added.

Lili's eyes were sparkling. "*You want* her with you?" A slow smile twitched at her lips. *"Quel hasard!"* she breathed. "What an adventure! It stirs the blood . . . but we shall not tell Henry!" She turned to Pomfret. "What do you think? Should we let the girl go with him?"

Pomfret faced the major's challenging gaze calmly. "I would say that Miss Lovelace will be safer with Major Norman until this situation is resolved than she would be with anyone else."

He was rewarded by a nod of thanks from Sly and a glowing smile from Moira.

Lili shrugged fatalistically. "You are all mad," she said, "I might as well accept it. Do you need another recruit?" and she chuckled.

Within a very short time Moira was clothed in a neat black woolen dress without any frills or furbelows to trouble her. A small black bonnet, part of her funeral costume, hid the bright hair; black gloves concealed her hands. The girl was comforted by the reminder of her dear parents. It was as though their love attended her, reinforcing, giving her strength for this desperate endeavor.

Lili and Pomfret saw them off quietly. The major stopped briefly at his own house. He did not let Moira accompany him inside, telling her firmly to *hold the horse* as he passed over the reins. Within a few minutes he was back beside her, dressed as soberly as she was, and took the reins to drive the small hooded vehicle through the early-afternoon traffic.

"No one will be able to recognize us in this excellent little carriage," Moira said happily.

"Cabriolet," corrected her companion. "It is an old-fashioned vehicle, but it does offer concealment, being both hooded and undistinguished. Adonis and his ilk would never allow themselves to be seen in such a plebeian turnout."

He is still sensitive to Adam Donat's sneers, the girl thought. Her voice was serene as she replied, "It is a perfect carriage for our purpose. Who would think a hero and a battlemaid would ride into deadly danger in such a quiet little coach? A perfect disguise!''

''They will take us for the vicar and his wife,'' agreed Sly casually.

Moira chuckled but did not pursue what was evidently a sore point with her soldier.

It was dusk by the time the major drew up in a country lane near a heavily wooded area. Removing the bars from a rustic gate, he drove the cabriolet into a field and then found a narrow cart track leading into the wood. Within minutes, they were advancing through virtual darkness. The major was silent, and Moira had no desire to interrupt his thoughts. After a slow and frustrating fifteen minutes, Moira discovered that the darkness in front of them was slightly less intense, and a few minutes more brought them in sight of an area marked by heaps of squared stone.

The ruins of which Mr. Beresford had told them!

Sly brought the cabriolet to a halt well within the shadow of the trees. He got out and led the tired horse back into the underbrush, turning him so that they could make a quick retreat if necessary. He placed a feed-bag over the horse's head, and then looked up at Moira.

The girl had been sitting quietly while her soldier made the arrangements. He stared up at her with admiration.

''It is a good soldier who knows enough to keep quiet at the proper times,'' he said. ''I am going to scout out the ruins now. I have a pistol, which is loaded, in my belt, and a knife in my boot, for defense. I am hoping I shall not have to use either of them. I tell you this, Moira, so you will know that I can protect myself, and that I have the power to rescue any victim. The Runners, as you know, are already converging on this place. The fact that we can neither see nor hear them is evidence of their training and skill.''

He waited, but Moira made no comment. The man went on, ''Do not be too alarmed if you hear a pistol shot. In such case, however, you will prepare our horse for a quick departure. Can you drive?''

190

"Yes," said Moira. "I have driven gigs and carts often—"

"In South Littlefield," finished Sly. "Thank God for your training in that excellent village!" He caught at her hand and brought it to his lips for a hard kiss. Then he stepped back from the cabriolet and vanished into the darkness of the wood. To rendezvous with the Runners, she hoped!

Moira sat very still, listening to the silence. After a moment she realized that it was not really silence. The night was filled with a number of very faint sounds. With relief the girl identified them: the noises of small animals, nesting birds, owls . . . sounds she had heard a thousand times in the village. . . .

Her tense muscles relaxed. She even smiled a little ruefully at her own image of herself fighting at the major's shoulder, defending his back from treacherous attacks. What arrogance on her part! Her duty was to wait here, alert for his signal, ready to drive out the moment he returned. Carefully she got down and went to the horse's head. He had finished his bait, and she removed the bag and stroked his neck gently. Then she returned to the cab and took up the reins, prepared to wait all night for her soldier if necessary.

The soldier moved silently through the night, seeking out shadowy cover as he approached the ruined chapel. There were other men somewhere near: he knew that with every battle-trained sense in his body. Some were allies, true; but there could be others, how many he did not know, who were hostile and ruthless.

He paused frequently in that stealthy advance, listening, peering, catching any scent that wafted through the quiet night. As he drew closer to the tumbled piles of stone, he caught a faint, deep droning resonance of men's voices. The very fact that they were audible told the soldier that the enemy had not yet sensed his own approach. With a silent rush, he brought himself into the shadow of the largest pile of slabs, his cheek pressed close against its cold rough surface. The voices—one voice—came more clearly. There was

191

a strange, wild note in it, a shrill threat that brought the hairs on the soldier's neck up in a frisson of warning.

"I told you—*no!*" cried the speaker. "When *I* am ready, the letter shall be sent. Not before!" There was tension in the tones, and unbearable strain. The speaker, thought Sly grimly, was either mad or whipping himself into a fury— to do *what*? At least one other man spoke, and then there was another low, uneven beat-and-pause of deep voices, in argument or pleading.

The soldier swung around the pile of slabs and saw before him the dark tunnel in the earth that had once been a stairway leading down into the crypt. It was from this hole that the voices now sounded more clearly.

"I may decide to punish you myself! You are all guilty, all stained with greed and treachery and dishonor . . . you deserve to die!" The voice broke in a choking gasp; there was the sound of a struggle, and then the thud of feet racing up the broken stairway.

Waiting no longer, the soldier launched himself toward the body that was erupting into the night.

A pistol shot sounded from the depths of the crypt.

After she had waited for what seemed like hours, Moira was surprised to note that the scene before her—the broad meadow with its tumbled, scattered piles of stone blocks— was becoming more visible. Surely it could not be dawn already! She blinked, and then noticed the silver-white glow rising above the eastern horizon. The moon was up. Moira debated whether this was a bad or good development. The major would be able to see more clearly, but then so would his antagonist! She twitched the reins gently, and the horse lifted his head and cocked his ears.

And then Moira heard the shot . . . and rapid footsteps. . . . Someone was running in her direction through the wood and trying to be very quiet. . . .

Gripping the reins convulsively, Moira held her breath. Let it be Hilary! she prayed, and leaned forward to give the horse the command to go the instant the major swung into the cabriolet.

CHAPTER TWENTY-FOUR

The footsteps abruptly halted.

Moira waited, hardly daring to breathe.

A large male body thrust itself up into the coach, pushing her backward.

"What the *hell*—!" snarled a voice she did not recognize. There was a tense moment as a hand came out and hit the firm round globes beneath the black wool bodice; hit, faltered—*stroked*. Then with a gasp, "Oh, I say! A thousand pardons, ma'am! I had no idea there was a lady . . . !"

"I'm waiting for my—husband," Moira explained in as prosaic a voice as she could summon up.

There was a charged silence. Then, in a voice quick with both incredulity and amusement, the intruder said mockingly, "At midnight? In the middle of a forest? Pull the other one, sweetheart!"

Since Moira's powers of invention had suddenly dried up, she remained silent.

The intruder heaved himself further into the cab, pushing Moira aside rudely to make room for his considerable bulk. "I am going to seek out the nearest constable. Would you have any idea where such might be found?"

"I do not believe you," Moira was annoyed at his discourteous attitude and behavior. "But if you really intend to find an officer of the law, there are at least ten Bow Street Runners in this immediate vicinity, any one of whom would be pleased to listen to your—story."

There was the sound of an indrawn breath. "*Runners?* Here?" and then, "Don't gammon me! I intend to have the truth! Just who are you?"

At that moment, in time to save Moira from having to invent any more lies, there came very clearly through the night the sound of another shot, and a distant chorus of shouts.

"By God, you meant it!" breathed the intruder. "Are they at the hunting lodge?"

"Yes," said Moira. Becoming a little confused in her efforts to get rid of the aggressive stranger, she said (loudly, so as to warn the major if he should be approaching), "You, sir, will stay here until you convince me you are on the side of the law."

"Don't tell me Bow Street is recruiting *women*!"

"I am not one of the Runners," said Moira crossly.

"For a camp-follower, you seem to know a good deal of what is going on." Sir John peered at the somberly clad female. Then he shrugged. "I may commandeer this grubby little vehicle to take me back to London. I've no desire to face Ado—my friend at the moment. He is convinced I betrayed him, and has threatened to kill me." He laughed. "Oh, I may as well relieve your fears. I am Sir John Benedict, and have just succeeded in escaping from a demmed, stinking cellar. I was supposed to find help and get back there before he killed them both." He laughed. "If the Runners have taken the fortress, I can be comfortable!"

Moira pushed at him fiercely. "Of course you cannot! What kind of a creature are you, to sit back doing nothing while your *best friend* is being murdered?" Then, as a hideous thought struck her, she gasped, "Or is it Adonis who is killing someone else?"

The brute had the discourtesy to laugh. "Oh, I don't *really* think so! Adam's got a devilish quick temper, but not enough venom to carry out a murder. Now, if we were speaking of that little weasel Vivian, I should not be so positive. He's a coward, but he's vicious, and hangs on like a leech to his grievances."

"Are you saying *Vivian* is the one who carried out this—crime?"

"Of course not! What odd ideas you women get! Vivian's badly hurt. He may be dead now, for all I know, or care. There hasn't been a word out of him for hours."

Moira had had enough. It was either succumb to hysteria or take violent action. Bending down, she unbuttoned one of her new shoes and, rising, hit the intruder hard on the head. Then, while he was shocked and in pain from the foul blow, she pushed him out of the cabriolet.

Benedict was cursing so loudly as he scrambled to his feet that he did not hear the rushing advance of the major. Hilary caught Sir John's shoulder, swung him around, and hit him so hard on the jaw that the nobleman went staggering back into the underbrush.

The major was up into the cabriolet and had the girl in his arms before a thankful Moira could control her emotions. "Are you safe, my darling? Did the brute hurt you?" he demanded.

"Oh, Hilary!" sobbed the girl. The word sounded so sweet on her tongue that she decided she would call him only by that name for the rest of their lives.

Her soldier laughed a little shakily. "I take it that means you are well," he said, kissing her. "We were successful in our raid on the hunting lodge. The Runners are cleaning up there now. I could not wait to get back to you, to be sure you were safe. And then to find you tussling with some fellow—!" He shook her gently and kissed her again.

"Tussling!" protested Moira. "I hit him with my new walking boot and pushed him out of our cabriolet! He was telling me that Vivian was dying, but he doesn't seem to be able to give a clear account of anything, except that his name is Benedict. You tell me, Hilary darling!"

Before the major could comply, a drawling voice sounded beside the coach. "So that's your husband, ma'am? I should have expected it!"

"And just what is *that* supposed to mean?" demanded the major, putting Moira safely behind him as he faced the intruder with cold belligerence.

Benedict hastened to apologize. "Both of you have pretty short fuses—er—I mean that the lady matches her partner in skill at arms," he explained. "I think I must consider myself fortunate to have escaped with only some bruises and a very sore head!"

The major accepted this handsome apology. "I have no doubt your recent ordeal in the crypt has rather put you off your pitch," he said graciously. "And my wife is a very special little battlemaid."

Benedict seemed to feel it was time he dropped that subject. He asked, "How went the battle? Was it you I ran into when I was breaking out of the crypt? I understand the Runners were with you?"

"We have the kidnapper under restraint," said the major in a quiet voice. "And I mean that literally. He is quite out of his senses, and has been so for some time, I gather from his other victims. He's kept you all tied up in that cellar, only giving you water but no food, while he *decided*—and I quote him—*how to punish the evildoers*."

"I know that much," agreed Sir John. "I was one of his demmed prisoners!"

"Along with Adam and Vivian Donat," the major told Moira. "He had them all tied up in that stinking cellar."

"But *who*? *Who*?" demanded Moira, sounding even to her own ears like a small owl.

The major grinned at her lovingly. "I believe the fellow's name is Hightower," he told her. "The marquess was in a fine fury when he found out who was at the bottom of the whole scheme. It seems Adam had already transferred Max Hightower's estate back to him legally, but the poor fellow was too confused to understand."

"Max had no need to get into such a pelter," sneered Sir John. "Everyone in London agrees that Adonis is the softest touch in town!"

"As *you*, sir, have good reason to know!" snapped Moira, unwisely.

"If a *man* had spoken to me thus—!" hissed Sir John.

The major laughed. "Consider that I did," he invited.

Sir John glared at him resentfully. "You know very well I cannot call you out."

"Meaning that I am too plebeian to soil your sword on?" asked the soldier unpleasantly.

"Meaning I probably owe you my life," grumbled the nobleman. "I heard that shot Max fired! It was your diversion at the head of the stairway that kept Hightower from following me out and gunning me down while I was trying to escape."

"Don't make me regret my generous action," advised the major with a reluctant grin.

For a moment Sir John appeared thunderstruck at this reprisal. Then he laughed and held out his hand. The two men shook hands firmly, and the major gave Sir John his name and rank.

Moira could not endure any more of male rituals. "If someone does not tell me exactly how this all came about, I shall simply drive away and leave you both to your little tête-à-tête!"

"Better that than doing us an injury." Benedict rubbed his head with a rueful grin. "Shall I tell her what I know?"

Before the major gave his consent, he mounted into the cab, pulled Moira close against him, and indicated that Sir John was to get in on the other side. "It will be a squeeze, but I must get Moira back to London before dawn." When they were settled, he headed the horse back toward the highroad and nodded to Benedict.

"Tell on."

It seemed that Max Hightower, never a stable man, had quite taken leave of his senses when he lost his family estate to Adam Donat. What with the mockery of his friends, the false condolences of his enemies, the outraged recriminations of his family, and his own chagrin, he had gone past the borders of reason into a world where it was proper for him to restore his lost fortunes by force. The strength of his emotions was understandable. Other gamesters, both male and female, had chosen to end their lives rather than face the results of their own poor judgment. So, drinking heavily and brooding over his folly, Max Hightower concocted a plan.

"He kidnapped me first," said Sir John, "since I was universally known to be the marquess's best friend. His plan was to hold me for ransom, exchanging me, in fact, for the wagered and lost estate." He smiled wryly. "I managed to retain enough of my wits to talk the fellow out of that idea."

"How did you manage that?" pressed Moira, plainly agog over the tale.

Sir John had the grace to look ashamed. "I persuaded Max that Vivian, as Adam's heir, would be a much stronger bargaining piece."

When there was no comment except a rather disapproving silence from his auditors, Benedict went on, "At that point my ploy went sour. Instead of releasing me, as I had expected, Hightower elected to keep us both. By this time I was urging him to write the note to Adam, demanding the return of Max's estates for the two of us, but his mind was—too disturbed. He kidnapped Adam."

Benedict shuddered. "Lying bound in that crypt . . . in the power of a madman . . . I cannot explain—! Hightower seemed to have forgotten his original scheme. He saw himself as the divinely appointed judge and custodian of all of us. Vivian cracked under the strain, and so constantly assaulted our ears with his complaints, accusations, and screams that Max struck him down to keep him quiet."

Sir John drew in a ragged breath. "Vivian wasn't dead, but Adam and I could see it might only be a matter of time. I had—had confessed to my part in the scheme—getting Vivian here in exchange for myself, and Adam of course was furious. I managed to get my hands loose and asked Adam to divert Max's attention while I tried to escape and bring help. And the rest you know," he concluded stiffly.

"They are taking all three—Vivian, Adam, and Max—to London right now," the major reassured the horrified girl. "Vivian will receive the best of care—and so will

Hightower, who seems to be sunk into a melancholy since the rescue of his victims.''

"Of course the fellow will receive only good treatment," Sir John added sententiously. "No one bears him a grudge for his insane folly. He may even recover in time," but his tone seemed to deny the possibility.

"He will recover faster if he is taken to his own home," Moira suggested. "To see the beloved, familiar sights around him, to realize that his home is indeed restored to him, will be the most effective medicine."

The major hugged her hard with his free arm, and Sir John said, "By Jove, you may be right!"

The major was fully occupied in piloting his small, crowded vehicle back to the London road in the dark, but he took time to glance admiringly down at his wise little comrade-at-arms. "She has a habit of being right," he grinned—that white, flashing, predatory smile that thrilled Moira, as the man well knew! "She chose me!"

Her answering smile glowed back at him. There was one problem that still nagged at her: the matter of Nims's death, but Moira decided to let well enough alone until she had her Hilary to herself.

At the point where the country lane met the main high-road, the cabriolet was stopped by a pair of armed officers from Bow Street. Major Norman offered his credentials, but the Runners politely refused them, asking that the gentleman and his party remain until the rest of the company caught up with them. It was all perfectly civil; not even Sir John felt able to ignore the request.

It seemed like an age to the weary trio but was actually only about half an hour before two heavy military-looking wagons pulled up at the temporary post. The marquess, incredibly rumpled and dirty after his ordeal in the crypt, tumbled out of the second wagon and strode over to the cabriolet.

"I understand I have you to thank for this rescue, Major Norman," he began stiffly. "You and Miss Lovelace found the vital clue that made our recovery possible, I am informed." And then, recognizing all three occupants of the small vehicle, his eyes opened wider. "Miss Lovelace! And *John*! Damn you, you traitor; what are you doing here, lolling at your ease? I told you to go for help!"

"I tried!" protested his friend. "Unfortunately, this lady was the occupant of the coach I had hoped to use. She hit me on the head with her boot."

All the men stared at the blushing Moira.

"My battlemaid," said the major, with pride and satisfaction.

The two noblemen regarded him with respect. And then Sir John made his third mistake of an unfortunate night.

"Your battlemaid, Major, I grant you that! But is this not the—ah—famous Miss Lovelace, of whom I have heard from Adam? I am sure it must be! Adonis's adoring wet-nurse and pet aversion? Suspect in the attacks upon him? Surely *she's* not your *wife*, Major?"

It was a close contest as to which of the outraged males would reach Benedict first. Adam was closest to his treacherous friend, and smarting at the ill-advised comments the fellow had babbled. The major, hampered by the fact that he was on the far side of the cab, and holding the reins, was delayed for a few crucial moments. By the time he had leaped to the ground and rounded the rear of the vehicle, Adam Donat had already done the job. Both men looked down at the limp, supine form, and the major said, "A neat facer!"

"He deserved it," growled Adonis. "*He* told that madman to kidnap Vivian and me!"

The men turned to take their places in the cabriolet. Moira climbed down to stand over the fallen body.

"Isn't someone going to pick him up? You cannot just leave him here, unconscious, in the middle of Surrey!"

"Oh, *no!*" groaned the Major, "not *another* rescue! My dearest idiot, *I love you*, but I *will not* have my future wife forever picking up wounded victims from the roadside! If you love me, you will get back into our cabriolet at once, and leave your detractor to the tender mercies of the local wildlife!"

200

"It would serve him right if that included tigers," added the marquess, dourly. "Traitor!"

Several of the Runners had been silent and appreciative witnesses of the whole scene. At this point one of them, no doubt anxious to get the wounded men back to London, stepped forward with an indulgent smile for Miss.

"I'll slip this one into the wagon and see him to London, if it will relieve the lady's mind," he offered.

"Thank you, officer," the major said in the crispest of parade-ground tones. "And you, Lord Donat, will accompany your friend in that same wagon, to make sure he gets safely home. *Is that understood, sir?*"

Even a dolt could see the folly of defying the major when he was in the military mode. Adam, no dolt but ever irrepressible, sketched a mocking salute and strode off after the Runners who were carrying the still-unconscious Benedict.

Moira found herself abruptly boosted into the small, enclosed space by a pair of hands that held her in a grip of iron. She decided to withhold comment upon this indignity until her wonderful soldier had had time to master his fears for her safety. Or whatever was making him so arrogantly masculine. When he had resumed his position beside her, he took her into his arms with savage tenderness.

"I had intended to tell you—*show you*—how necessary I find your presence here beside me tonight, after the battle we have shared." He kissed her, his passion gently tempered with concern for her weariness. "Sweetheart, you must be exhausted. It is time I got you safe home to Lili." Raising his head from the sweetest lips he had ever known, the major settled his dear girl cozily against him, and started the drive to London.

"Go to sleep, my darling," he said softly.

EPILOGUE

Three weeks later they were married in the old stone church in South Littlefield by a beaming Reverend Clarence. Lili and Henry graced the ceremony, and so did Mr. Samuel Beresford. The groom was splendid in his dress uniform. He had received an offer from Mr. Pitt to join his staff as adviser, which could not be refused, and was now confident he could support his new wife in a manner that pleased him mightily. While he waited for his bride to come to him, he slanted a look at Henry Hassleton, looking very self-satisfied in the front pew, friends of the bride side.

Henry had surprised even himself by the generosity of the dowry he had insisted upon providing for Moira. If it had not been for her, Henry reminded himself, he would never have had the idea of restoring the guildhall—a plan that was bringing him more rewards than even he had dared to hope for. Lost in dreams of Henry Hassleton, lord mayor of London, he was scarcely aware of where he was. Lili will look out for him, thought the bridegroom cheerfully. Just as I shall look after my dearest heart, my little battle-maid! the soldier vowed.

It was not until some days later that Moira remembered to ask her new husband how the spy Nims had met his death.

"Mr. Pitt told me that Nims had been discovered to be a double traitor, dealing with both Napoleon and Pitt, and

202

betraying both. I learned that his death had something to do with those activities,'' the major explained.

In the soldier's memory sounded the quiet voice: *"I am taking you off this business. C will handle the kill."* A detail he could not in honor reveal even to his wife.

"Which explains the turned coat," she was agreeing. "But what had his letter addressed to Donat to do with the matter?"

"Probably nothing at all," answered the major, nuzzling her throat. "Nims was greedy. The note was likely part of a blackmail scheme he was working on at the time of his death." He raised his head and gave her a rueful glance. "Real life doesn't always tie up all the ends neatly, my darling."

He brought her close against his warm, hard body and kissed her. "Do we *have* to talk about him at this moment, sweetheart? On our *honeymoon*?"

He sounded so much like a charming boy that Moira's foolish heart melted into honeyed warmth. "I *can* think of more pleasurable activities," she admitted lovingly, stroking his strong, muscled chest with provocative fingertips. Oh, the joy of making free of this splendid male body— the comfort, the pleasure! From the beginning she had found it easy to be open—even daring—with this man; easy to laugh, to make absurd jokes. He would never reject her, never hurt her, never allow her to be hurt.

"I am the most fortunate woman in the world," she said.

Hilary's laugh was a shout of delight. "That is true, of course," he said, his eyes alight with love and mischief. And then, complacently, he commanded, "Tell me more."

His new wife looked at him with such love in her face that the man grew suddenly still.

"There is," Moira quoted the Reverend Clarence, "a time to talk—and a time to love."

"Oh, yes!" breathed the soldier, and took her into his arms.

Romance

and

Intrigue

from the ever popular...

Elizabeth Chater

Available at your bookstore or use this coupon.

____THE KING'S DOLL	20084	2.25
____THE REFORMED RAKE	20083	2.25
____THE MARRIAGE MART	20082	2.25
____A SEASON FOR THE HEART	50238	1.50
____GALLANT LADY	50217	1.50
____THE DUKE'S DILEMMA	20749	2.50
____MILADY HOT-AT-HAND	21176	2.50

FAWCETT MAIL SALES
Dept. TAF, 201 E. 50th St., New York, N.Y. 10022

Please send me the FAWCETT BOOKS I have checked above. I am enclosing $....................(add 50¢ per copy to cover postage and handling). Send check or money order—no cash or C.O.D.'s please. Prices and numbers are subject to change without notice. Valid in U.S. only. All orders are subject to availability of books.

Name_____

Address_____

City_____State_____Zip Code_____

14   Allow at least 4 weeks for delivery.   TAF-38